BOB BOOKS®

Developing Readers

Workbook

Ask for Bob Books® at your local bookstore, or visit www.bobbooks.com.

ISBN 978-1-338-22679-9

10 9 8 7 6 5 4 3 2 1   18 19 20 21 22

Printed in the U.S.A. 08

First printing 2018

Developing Readers
Workbook

Bob Books: Word Families
Workbook Activities

Book 1: Floppy Mop 10

Book 2: Lolly Pops 18

Book 3: Frogs 26

Book 4: The Red Car 34

Book 5: Summer 42

Book 6: Kittens 50

Book 7: Funny Bunny 58

Book 8: Bed Bugs 66

I read it! Checklist 75

My Book Report 77

I read it! Certificate 79

Bob Books: Complex Words
Workbook Activities

Book 1: Ten Men 82

Book 2: Bump! 90

Book 3: Cat and Mouse 98

Book 4: The Swimmers 106

Book 5: Samantha 114

Book 6: Willy's Wish 122

Book 7: Jumper and the Clown 130

Book 8: Max and the Tom Cats 138

I read it! Checklist 147

My Book Report 149

I read it! Certificate 151

Bob Books: Long Vowels
Workbook Activities

Book 1: The Game 154

Book 2: Joe's Toe 162

Book 3: Bud's Nap 170

Book 4: The Picnic 178

Book 5: The Train 186

Book 6: The Visit 194

Book 7: Chickens 202

Book 8: The King 210

I read it! Checklist 219

My Book Report 221

I read it! Certificate 223

Word Families

Workbook Activities

Use **cat** **sat**, and **is** to complete each sentence. Then read the story and color each picture.

Mop was Tom's pal.

Tom _sat_ on Mop.

Jack was a _cat_.

Zack was a rat.

Mop ran after Jack and Zack.

Mop and Tom _sat_.

Color Tom, Mop, Jack, and Zack.
Who sat on Mop?   ToM

Mop was Tom's pal.

Zack ran. Jack ran
after Zack.

Floppy Mop

Circle and write the correct word.

(pal) gal

Pal

Zack   Sack

Zack

happy   floppy

Floppy

stop   flop

Stop

cap   nap

nap

Tom   Mom

Tom

Find and color the hidden word. Then draw a line to the matching picture.

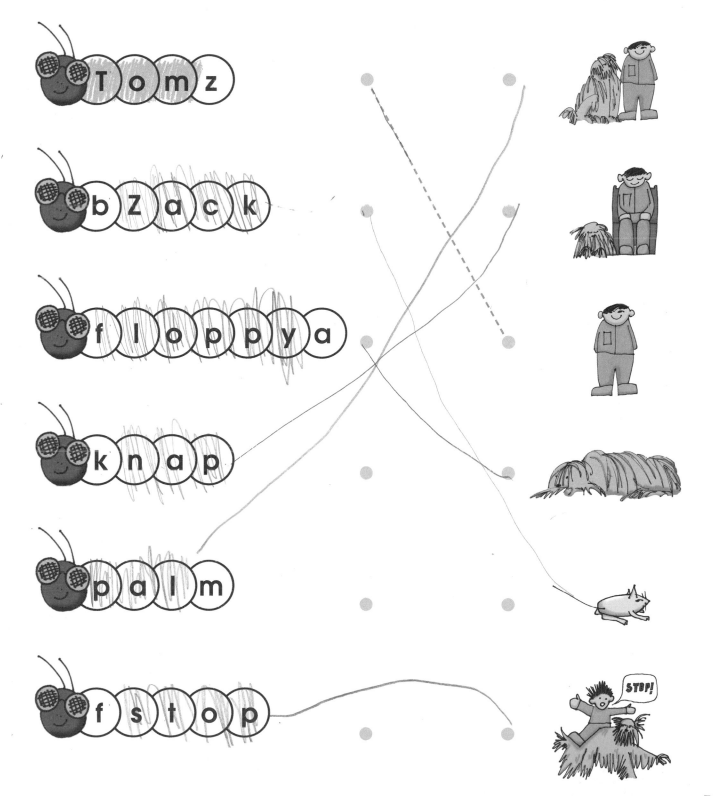

T o m z

b Z a c k

f l o p p y a

k n a p

p a l m

f s t o p

Floppy Mop

Find the sight words and color them to match the key below. Count how many you found.

| a | was | said | come | after |

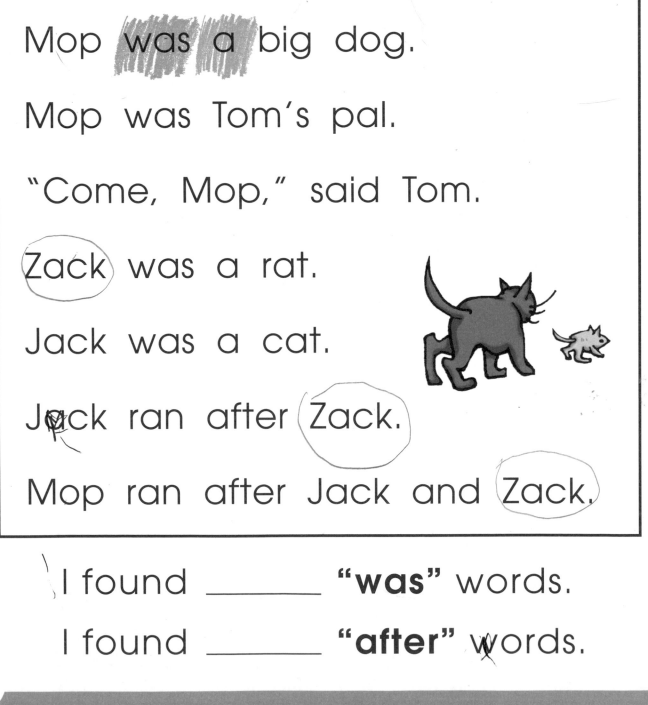

Mop was a big dog.

Mop was Tom's pal.

"Come, Mop," said Tom.

Zack was a rat.

Jack was a cat.

Jack ran after Zack.

Mop ran after Jack and Zack.

I found _____ **"was"** words.

I found _____ **"after"** words.

Circle and write the correct word to match the picture.

Mop was a big dog.
(big   dig)

_____ was a cat.
(Sack   Jack)

_____ was a rat.
(Pack   Zack)

Mop was _____ pal.
(Tom's   Mom's)

Mop was a _____ dog.
(sloppy   floppy)

 Read, say, and write the words.

pal  pal

nap  nap

Tom  Tom

floppy  floppy

Zack

stop

Write the words in the correct order to make the sentences.

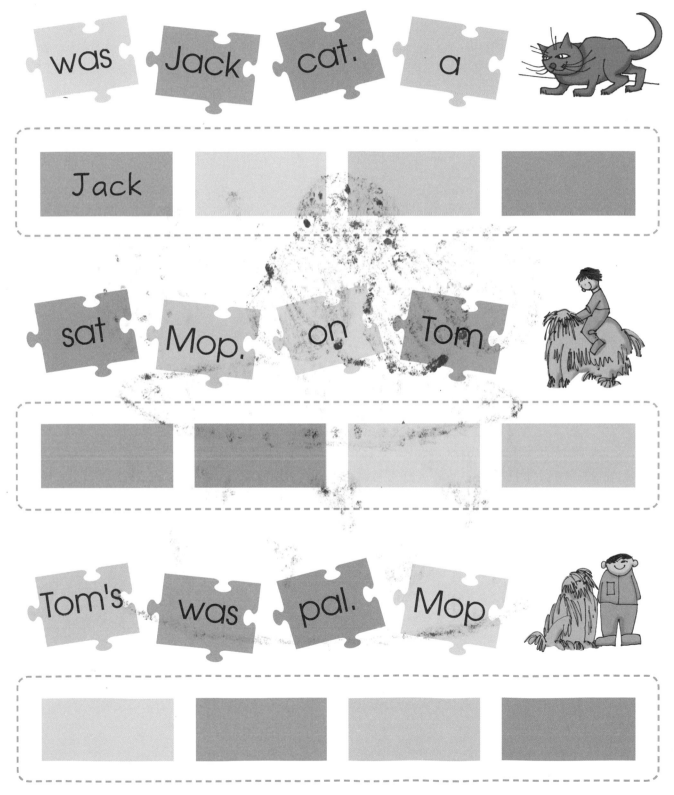

was Jack cat. a

Jack

sat Mop. on Tom

Tom's was pal. Mop

 Color the lolly-pops.
How many lolly-pops do you see? ___6___

Lolly-Pops

Use **shop** and **was** to complete each sentence. Then read the story and color each picture.

Polly _____ a jolly bird.

Polly flapped. Polly bobbed.

Polly sat on Dolly.

Dolly and Jon went to a _____.

The _____ had lolly-pops.

Dolly and Jon got lolly-pops.

 Circle and write the correct word.

(flap)   snap

_____

stop   shop

_____

Polly   Dolly

_____

new   flew

_____

molly   lolly-pop

_____

Dolly   jolly

_____

Find and color the hidden word. Then draw a line to the matching picture.

Lolly-Pops

 Find the sight words and color them using the key below. Count how many you found.

| to | wants | was | said | a |

Polly was a jolly bird.

"Hello, Polly," said Jon.

Polly flew to Dolly.

Dolly and Jon went to a shop.

"Polly wants a lolly-pop."

"Yum, yum!" said Polly.

I found _____ **"to"** words.

I found _____ **"said"** words.

Circle and write the correct word to match the picture.

The _____ had lolly-pops.

(shop   stop)

Dolly and _____ went to a shop.

(Jon   Jin)

Polly _____ .

(flapped   snapped)

Dolly had _____ pennies.

(ten   men)

"Yum, _____ ,!" said Dolly.

(mum   yum)

Lolly-Pops

 Write the words in the correct order to make the sentences.

flew   Dolly.   Polly   to

sat   Polly   Dolly.   on

six   Jon   pennies.   had

Read, say, and write the words.

flap  flap

Polly  Polly

lolly-pop  lolly-pop

shop  shop

Dolly  Dolly

flew  flew

 Color the polliwogs and frogs.
How many polliwogs do you see? _____

Polliwogs

Frogs

Use **frogs**, **jump**, and **big** to complete each sentence. Then read the story and color each picture.

Ten polliwogs swam in the pond.

The bird was _____ and tall.

The bird saw the polliwogs and _____.

"Jump! Hide!" said Papa.

"_____! Dive!" said Mama.

The frogs went under a log.

Frogs

(pond) bond

slim   swim

third   bird

wonder   under

small   tall

frog   hog

Find and color the hidden word. Then draw a line to the matching picture.

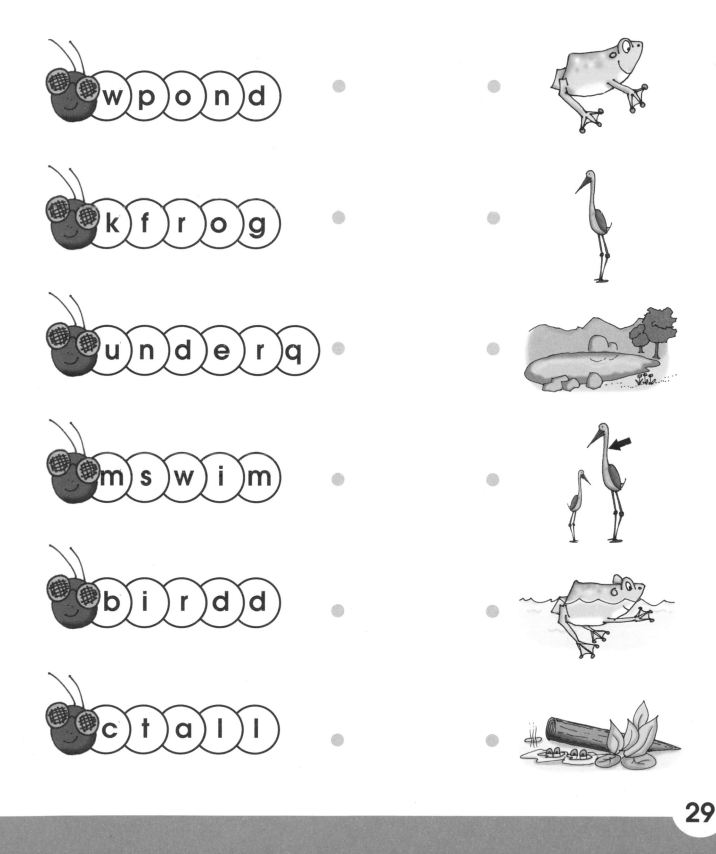

w p **o n d**

k **f r o g**

u n d e r q

m **s w i m**

b i r d d

c **t a l l**

Frogs

 Find the sight words and color them to match the key below. Count how many you found.

| bird | a | went | the | was |

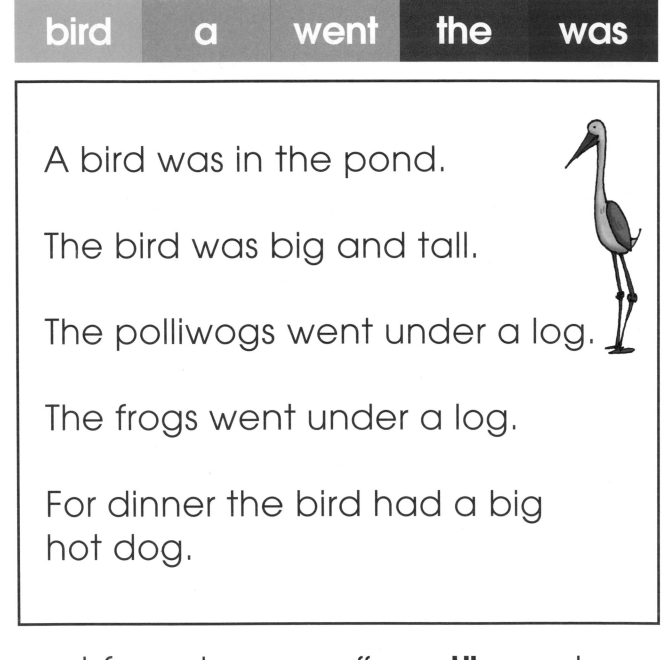

A bird was in the pond.

The bird was big and tall.

The polliwogs went under a log.

The frogs went under a log.

For dinner the bird had a big hot dog.

I found _____ **"went"** words.

I found _____ **"the"** words.

Circle and write the correct word to match the picture.

The bird was _____ and tall.

(big   pig)

The polliwogs _____
under a log.

(bent   went)

The frogs went under

a _____.

(hog   log)

_____! Hide!

(Pump   Jump)

The bird saw the polliwogs
and _____.

(frogs   smogs)

 Read, say, and write the words.

pond

bird

under

frog

swim

tall

Put the words in the correct order to make a sentence.

the | bird | The | saw | frogs.

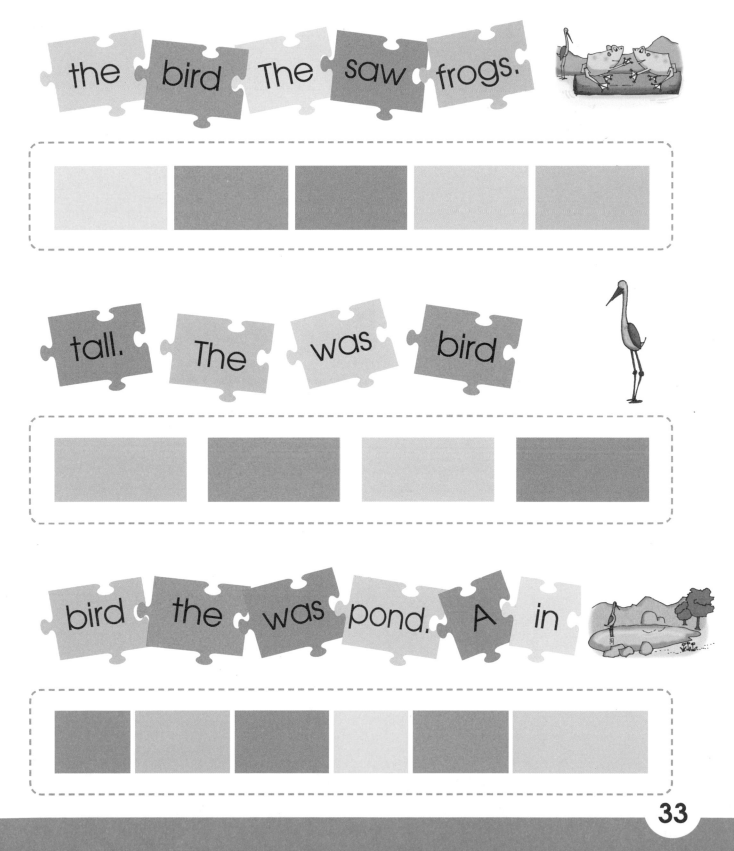

tall. | The | was | bird

bird | the | was | pond. | A | in

33

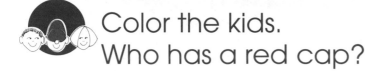 Color the kids.
Who has a red cap? _____

The Red Car

Carl   Mark   Barb

Use **start** and **star** to complete the sentences. Then read the story and color each picture.

Barb had a red car.

The car was a _____.

The red car did not _____.

Mark hopped out.
Carl hopped out.

The car started.

Barb, Mark, and Carl sped off in the red car.

The Red Car

Circle and write the correct word.

(push)   cash

_____

Bark   Barb

_____

car   far

_____

star   jar

_____

mart   smart

_____

start   part

_____

36

Find and color the hidden word. Then draw
a line to the matching picture.

l p u s h

c a r p

f s t a r

t s m a r t

B a r b b

s t a r t q

The Red Car

 Find and color the sight words.
Count how many you found.

will   **we**   **out**   **was**   **said**

The red car was a star.

Mark hopped out.

Carl hopped out.

"We will push the car," said Mark and Carl.

"Smart!" said Barb.

I found _____ **"out"** words.

I found _____ **"said"** words.

Circle and write the correct word to match the picture.

Barb had a _____ car.

(red   bed)

The car _____ .

(man   ran)

Barb sat in the _____ .

(star   car)

The car did not _____ .

(start   smart)

"Hop in, Mark.
_____ in, Carl," said Barb.

(Hop   Pop)

The Red Car

 Put the words in the correct order to make a sentence.

out. Mark hopped

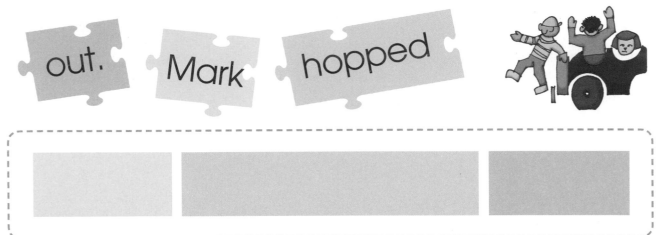

a The star. car was

car started. The

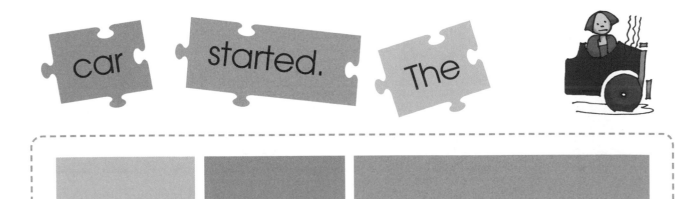

 Read, say, and write the words.

push  *push*

star ⭐

car

start

Barb

smart

 Color the sun.
Color the tree.
What is your favorite season? _____

| summer   fall   winter   spring |

Summer

Use **pond** and **hot** to complete the sentences. Then read the story and color each picture.

It was _____.

Molly and Mom went to the _____.

Ducks swam in the pond.
Fish swam in the pond.

Molly put her toes in the pond.

Molly and Mom jumped into the pond.

Molly and Mom sat in the pond.
The sun was _____, but the pond was not.

Summer

Use a word from the word bank to fill in the boxes.

Word Bank

Molly   red   duck   fish   hot   Mom

h	o	t

Write the letters from the colored boxes.

44

Find and color the hidden word. Then draw a line to the matching picture.

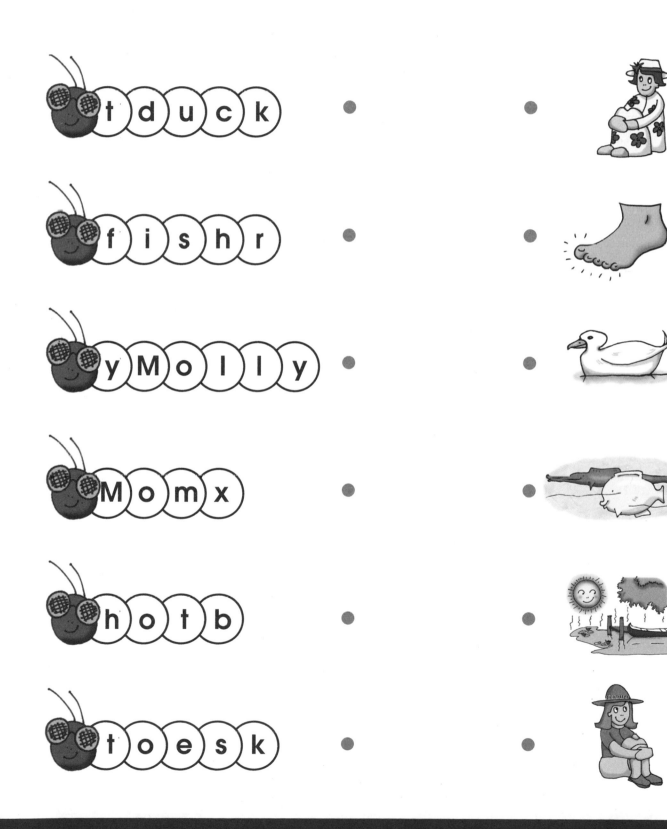

t d u c k

f i s h r

y M o l l y

M o m x

h o t b

t o e s k

 Color the bubbles with the word "**her**" red.
Color the bubbles with the word "**into**" blue.
Color the bubbles with the word "**put**" orange.
Use these words to finish the sentences.

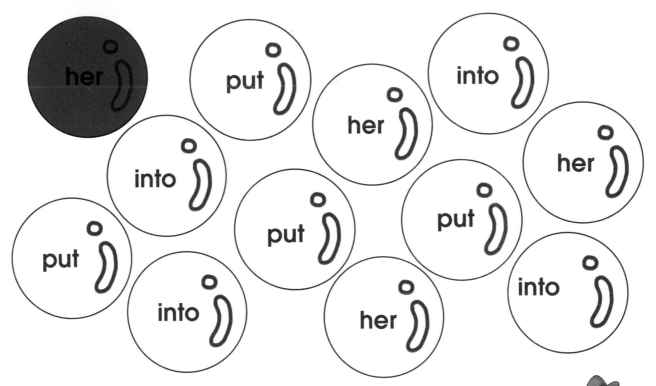

Mom _____ her hands in the pond.

Molly put _____ toes in the pond.

Molly and Mom jumped _____ the pond.

46

Circle and write the correct word to match the picture.

It was _____ .

(pop   hot)

Molly had a big _____ .

(cat   hat)

_____ swam in the pond.

(Ducks   Trucks)

Molly and _____ sat in the pond.

(Tom   Mom)

Molly and Mom _____ .

(jumped   pumped)

47

 Put the words in the correct order to make the sentences.

was   hot   It

_____ _____ _____ _____ _____ h_____ .

pond   sat   the   They   in

_____ _____ _____ s_____ _____ _____ _____

t_____ _____ _____ .

swam   the   Fish   in   pond

_____ _____ _____ s_____ _____ _____ _____

_____ _____ p_____ .

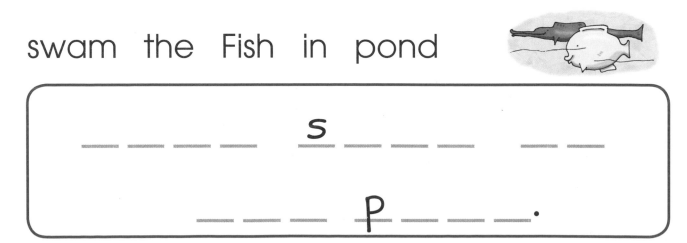

Read, say, and write the words.

Molly  Molly

toes

duck

fish

hot

Mom

 Color the kittens.
How many kittens do you see? _____
What is your favorite pet? _____.

| dog | cat | bird | hamster | fish | horse |

Kittens

Use **bed** and **luck** to complete the sentences. Then read the story and color each picture.

Jill met a big cat.

Jill was sad.
Cat was sad.

"What is the matter?"
said Jim.

"The cat had bad
_____," said Jill.

"I saw six kittens
in my _____," said Bill.

The cat was happy.

Kittens

Use a word from the word bank to fill in the boxes.

Word Bank

kittens   call   ran   six   happy   luck

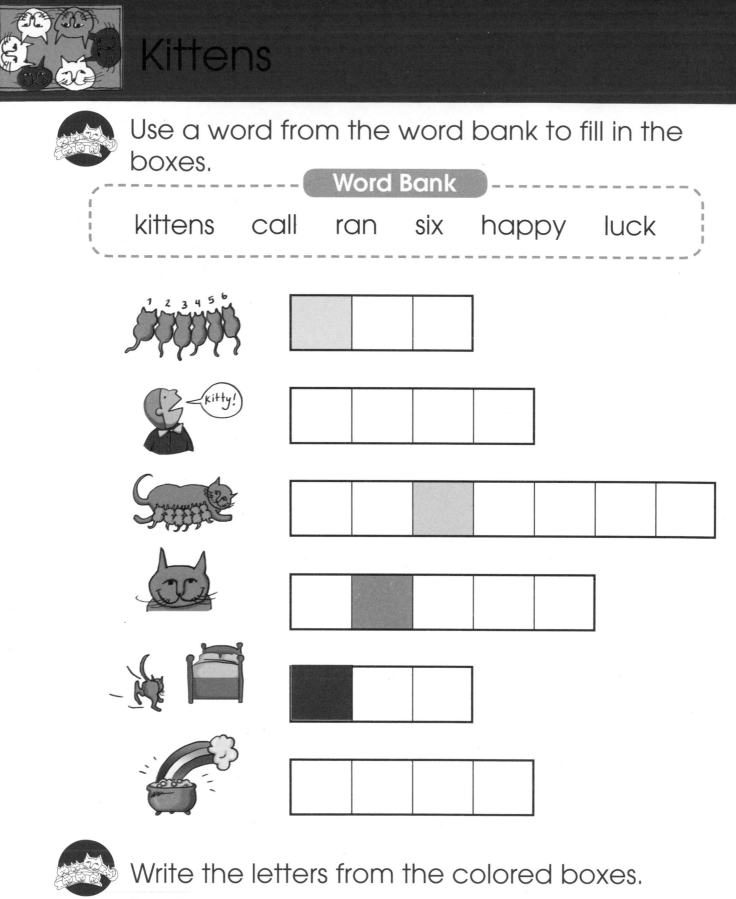

Write the letters from the colored boxes.

Find and color the hidden word. Then draw a line to the matching picture.

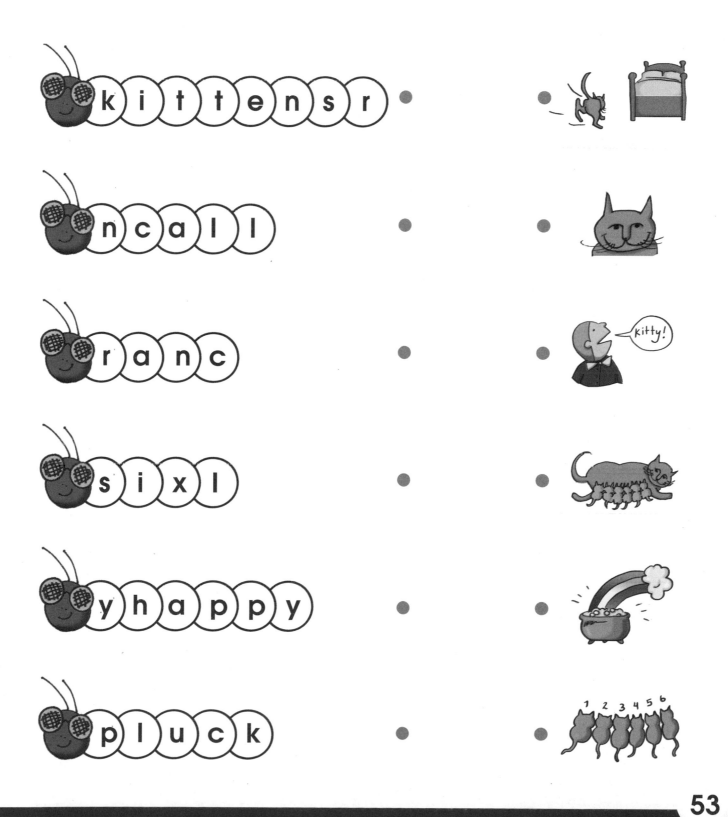

k i t t e n s r

n c a l l

r a n c

s i x l

y h a p p y

p l u c k

Kittens

 Color the cats with the word "**her**" purple.
Color the cats with the word "**are**" yellow.
Color the cats with the word "**saw**" blue.
Use these words to finish the sentences.

her   are   saw

saw   her

are   her   saw

The cat has lost _____ kittens.

The cat and Jill and Jim _____ sad.

"I _____ six kittens in my bed," said Bill.

54

Circle and write the correct word to match the picture.

Jill met a _____ cat.

(big   dig)

Jill and Cat were _____ .

(sad   mad)

"The cat had _____ luck," said Jill.

(dad   bad)

"I saw _____ kittens in my bed," said Bill.

(mix   six)

Jill and Jim and Cat ran to Bill's _____ .

(bed   red)

 Put the words in the correct order to make the sentences.

big   a   met   Jill   cat

_____ _____ _____ _____ _____ _____ b_____ _____

_____ _____ _____ .

sad   Jill   was

_____ _____ _____ _____ _____ s_____ _____ .

was   The   happy   cat

_____ _____ _____ t_____ _____ _____

_____ _____ _____ .

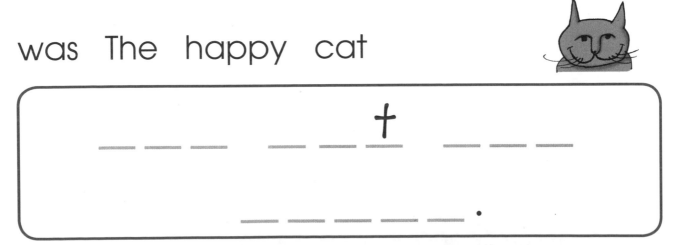

Read, say, and write the words.

kittens  _kittens_

call

ran

six

happy

luck

Color the bunnies.
What are they doing? _____

Funny Bunny

Use **run**, **fox**, and **luck** to complete the sentences. Then read the story and color each picture.

Tup and Tip had fun.

Lox the _____ was hungry.

"The fox is cunning. The fox wants us for supper. _____!" said Tup.

But the fox ran fast.

The fox was out of _____ .

Tip and Tup had carrots and turnips for supper.

Funny Bunny

Use a word from the word bank to fill in the boxes.

Word Bank

run   up   down   fox   fun   fast

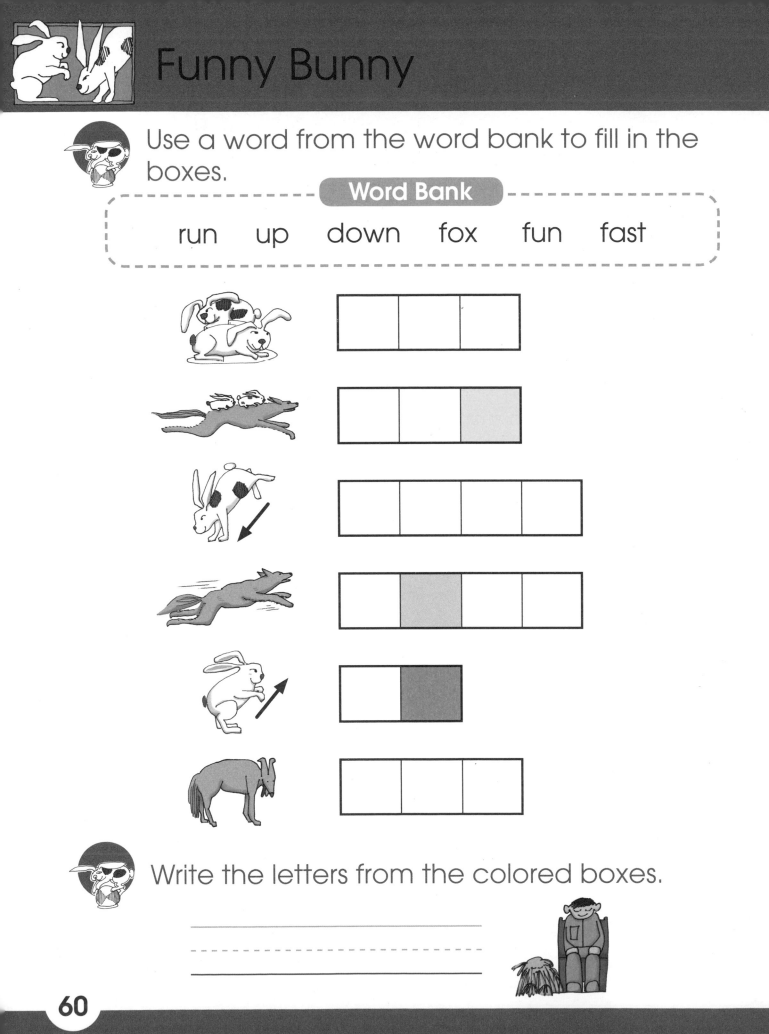

Write the letters from the colored boxes.

_____

_____

Find and color the hidden word. Then draw a line to the matching picture.

p r u n

i u p j

d o w n f

k f o x

b f u n l

f a s t w

Color the balls with the word "**did**" orange.
Color the balls with the word "**out**" green.
Color the balls with the word "**went**" red.
Use these words to finish the sentences.

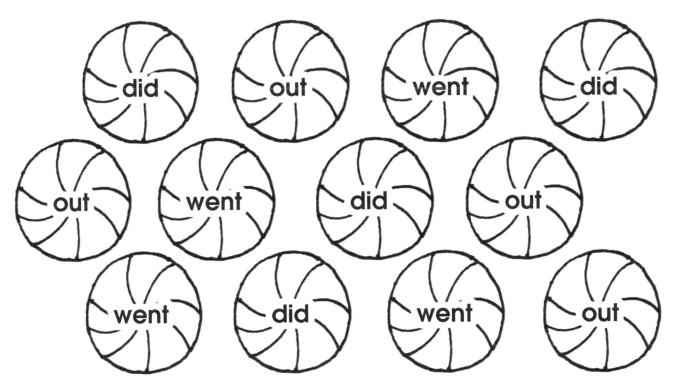

Tup and Tip _____ stunts.

"Puff, puff, puff," _____ the fox.

The fox was _____ of luck.

62

Circle and write the correct word to match the picture.

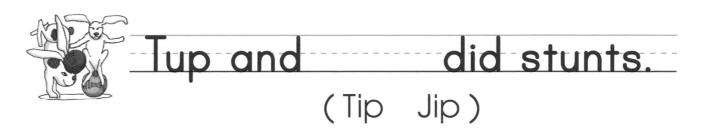

Tup and _____ did stunts.

(Tip   Jip)

Tup and Tip had _____ .

(fun   sun)

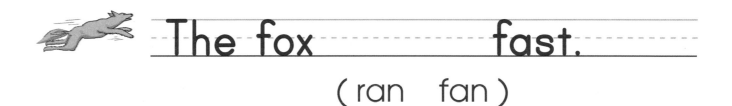

The fox _____ fast.

(ran   fan)

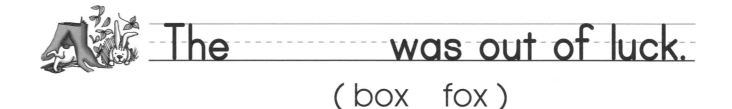

The _____ was out of luck.

(box   fox)

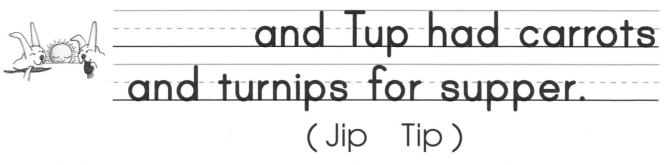

_____ and Tup had carrots
and turnips for supper.

(Jip   Tip)

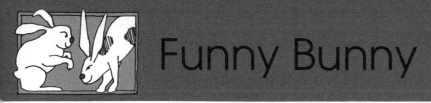

Funny Bunny

 Put the words in the correct order to make the sentences.

fox   ran   The   fast

f _ _ _   _ f _ _   _ _ _

_ _ _ _ _ .

hungry   The   fox   was

_ _ _   _ _ _   w _ _

_ _ _ _ _ _ _ .

jumped   down   Tup

u _ _   _ u _ _ _ _

_ _ _ _ .

Read, say, and write the words.

run  _run_

up

down

fox

fun

fast

 Color the clock.
What time is it? _____

bong
bong
bong
bong
bong

bong
bong
bong
bong
bong

Use **clock**, **end**, and **up** to complete the sentences.
Then read the story and color each picture.

The _____ struck ten.

Meg and Fred were
sent to bed.

Fred jumped _____.

Papa was upset.
Mama was upset.

Meg and Fred jumped and
the big bed fell.

That was the _____ of
jumping on the bed.

Bed Bugs

Use a word from the word bank to fill in the boxes.

Word Bank

bend   Fred   head   upset   rest   clock

Write the letters from the colored boxes.

_____

- - - - - - - - - - - - - - - -

68

Find and color the hidden word. Then draw
a line to the matching picture.

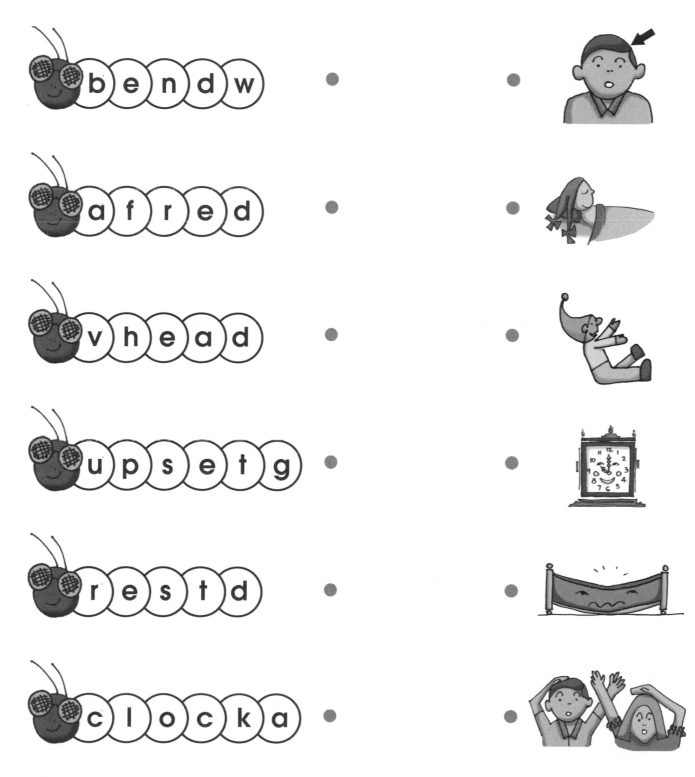

Bed Bugs

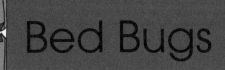 Color the beds with the word "**on**" purple.
Color the beds with the word "**down**" green.
Color the beds with the word "**all**" red.
Use these words to finish the sentences.

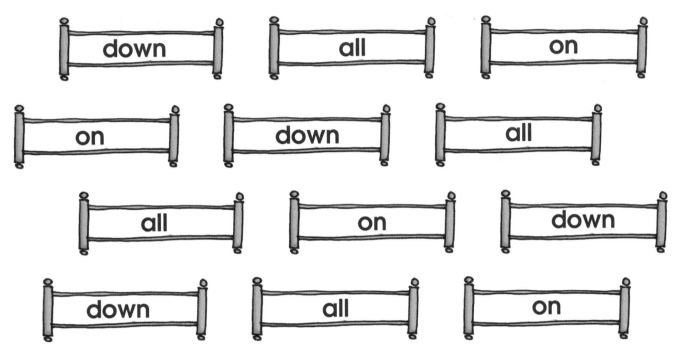

down	all	on
on	down	all
all	on	down
down	all	on

Fred and Meg jumped
_____the bed.

Meg jumped _____.

Papa said,
"Hush _____ that fuss."

Circle and write the correct word to match the picture.

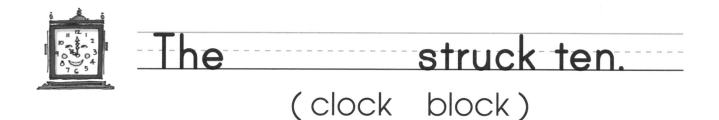

The _____ struck ten.

(clock   block)

jumped up.

(Sled   Fred)

Fred felt the bed _____.

(bend   send)

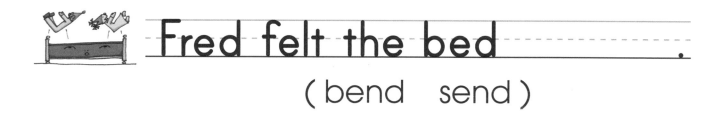

Meg felt the bed _____.

(bump   pump)

 Papa said, "Hush all that _____."

(muss   fuss)

71

Bed Bugs

Put the words in the correct order to make the sentences.

ten   struck   The   clock

c

.

jumped   Fred   up

r

.

was   upset   Papa

u

.

Read, say, and write the words.

bend  *bend*

Fred

head

upset

rest

clock

I read it!

Word Families

1. ☐ Floppy Mop

2. ☐ Lolly-Pops

3. ☐ Frogs

4. ☐ The Red Car

5. ☐ Summer

6. ☐ Kittens

7. ☐ Funny Bunny

8. ☐ Bed Bugs

My Book Report

Name: _____ **Date:** _____

Name
The title of my book is...

Characters
The main characters are...

Book Rating
I give the book...

☆ ☆ ☆ ☆ ☆

Setting
This story takes place in...

Beginning

→

Middle

→

End

My favorite part of the book is...

_____

_____

_____

Make a copy of this page for each of the books in the set.

"I read the whole book!"

BOB BOOKS
Word Families

_____

Name

Complex Words

Workbook
Activities

Ten Men

Read the story and color each picture. Then circle the words in each sentence that have a short "e" sound, as in "hen."

Ten Men

Hand in hand they went.

They went in wind.

They went in sand.

Into a tent
the ten men went.

The sun has set on
the ten and the tent.

Say and write the words.

tent   *tent*

flag

end

drum

hand

wind

Ten Men

Read each clue and complete the crossword.

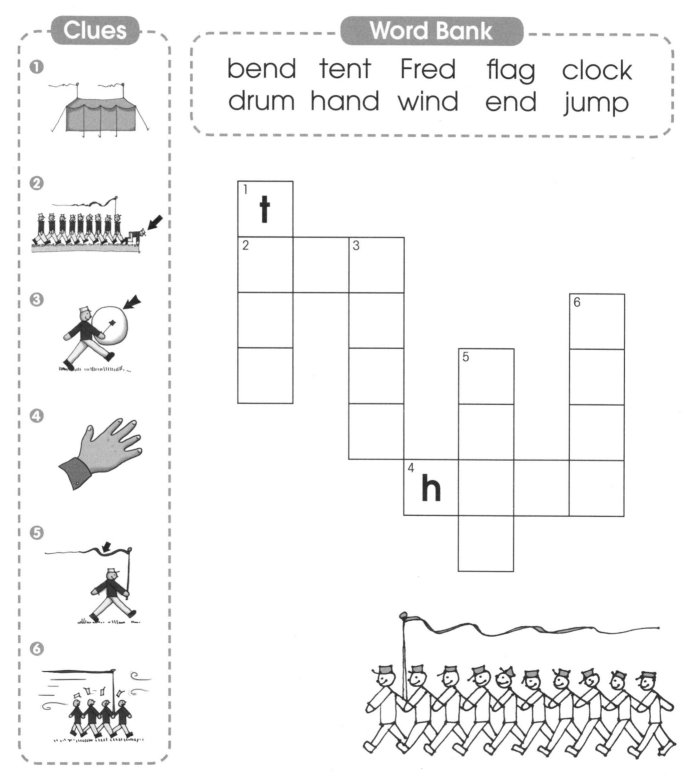

Clues

1
2
3
4
5
6

Word Bank

bend tent Fred flag clock
drum hand wind end jump

Fill in the missing letters to complete the sentences.

They went in wi___ ___.

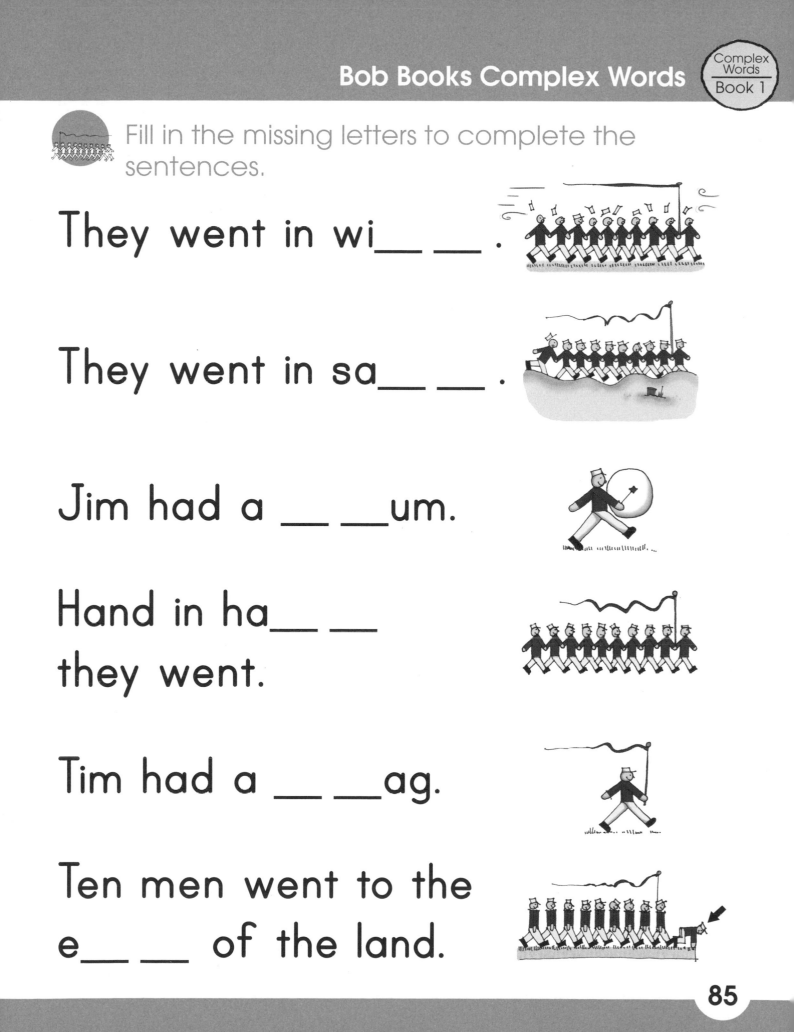

They went in sa___ ___.

Jim had a ___ ___um.

Hand in ha___ ___
they went.

Tim had a ___ ___ag.

Ten men went to the
e___ ___ of the land.

Ten Men

Circle the words with the **short "e"** sound. Connect the circles to make a path.

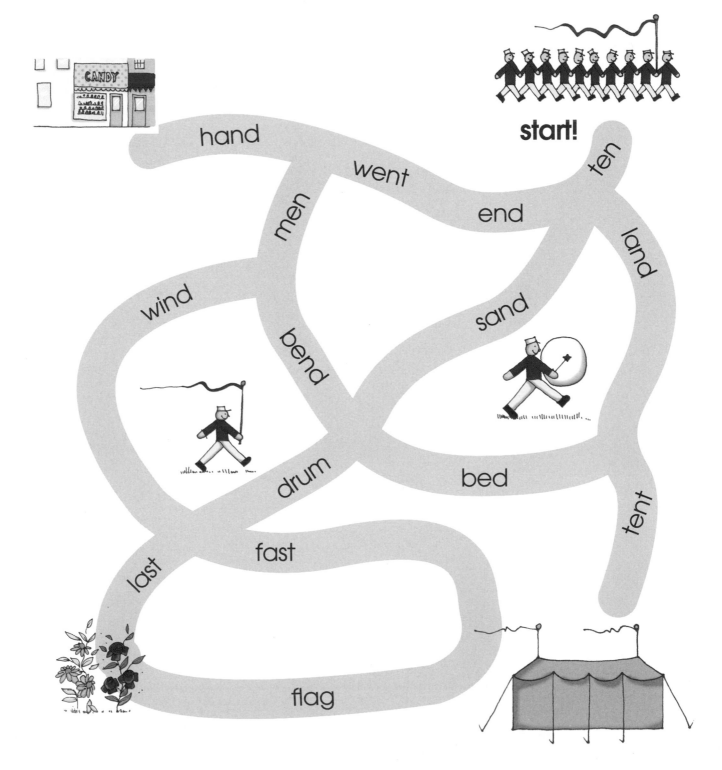

start!

hand

went

ten

end

men

land

wind

sand

bend

drum

bed

fast

last

tent

flag

CANDY

Draw a line to the correct word, then write it.

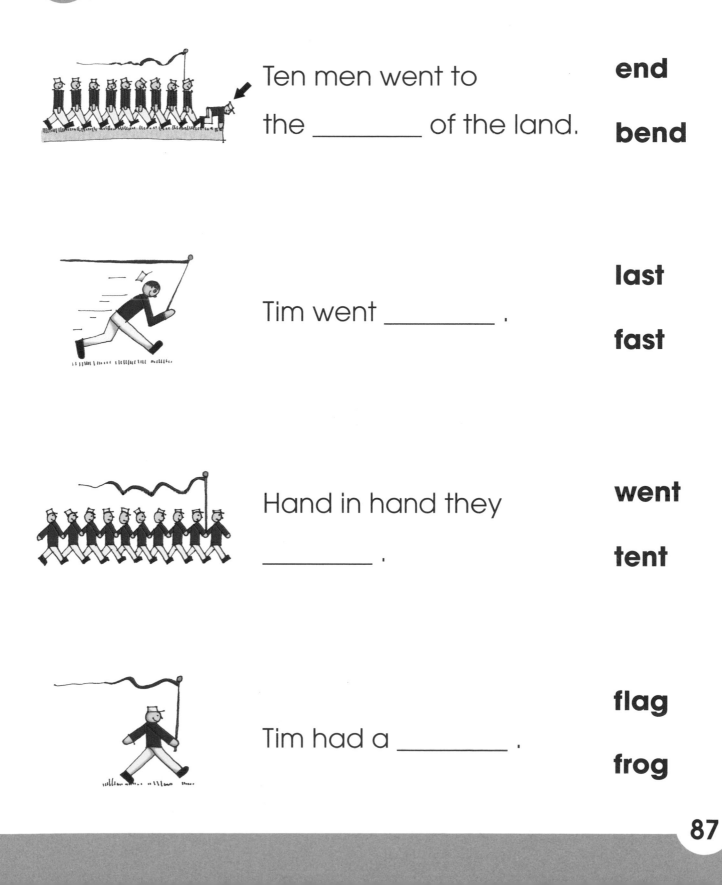

Ten men went to
the _____ of the land.

end

bend

Tim went _____ .

last

fast

Hand in hand they
_____ .

went

tent

Tim had a _____ .

flag

frog

Ten Men

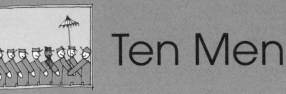

Make complete sentences using the words from box A and box B.

Box A

Tim

They

Jim

Box B

went in sand.

had a drum.

went fast.

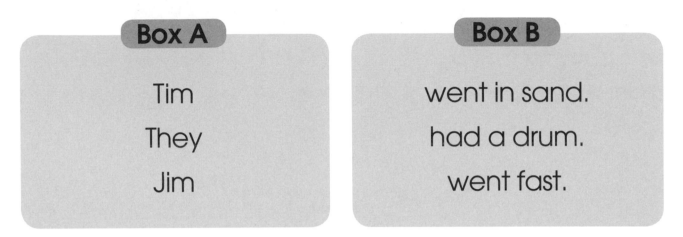

Draw a line from each picture to the correct consonant blend. Fill in the blank.

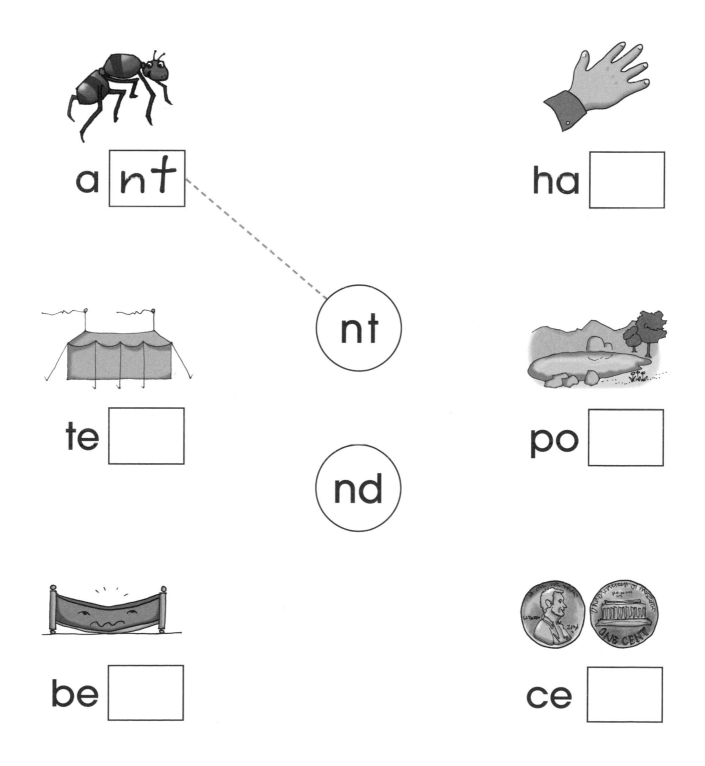

a nt

ha ☐

te ☐

nt

po ☐

nd

be ☐

ce ☐

Bump!

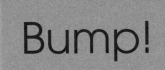

Read the story and color each picture. Then circle the words in each sentence that have a short "u" sound, as in "bug."

Bump!

Sunny jumped.

Skipper and Thumper bumped!

Sunny and Thumper jumped up.

Skipper slipped.

Jimmy and Skipper skipped.

Say and write the words.

bump   _bump_

jump

slip

over

Thumper

Jimmy

Bump!

Read each clue and complete the crossword.

Clues

1
2
3
4
5
6

Word Bank

six bump up slip Thumper
over fish jump fun Jimmy

Fill in the missing letters to complete the sentence.

Sunny ju__ __ed.

Thumper skipp__ __.

Skipper __ __ipped.

Skipper and Thumper
bu__ __ed!

__ __umper jumped.

Bump!

 Circle the words with the **short "u"** sound.
Connect the circles to make a path.

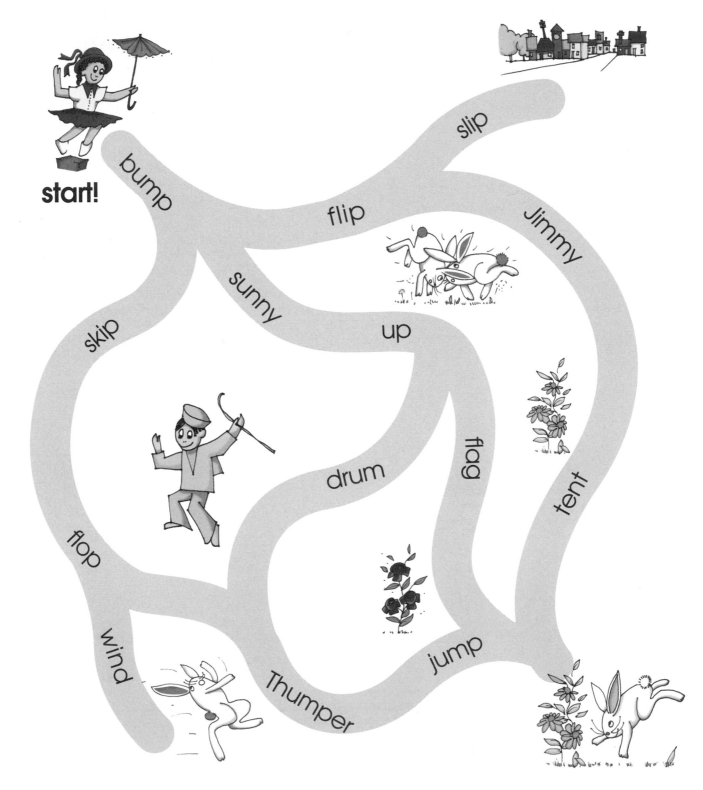

start!

bump

slip

flip

Jimmy

sunny

up

skip

flag

tent

flop

drum

wind

Thumper

jump

Draw a line to the correct word, then write it.

Jimmy _____ .

jumped

bumped

Skipper jumped
and _____ .

dripped

skipped

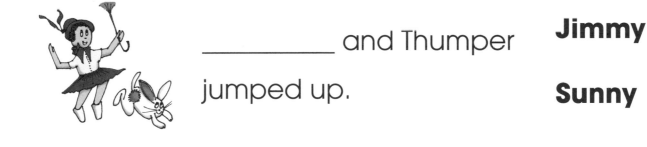

_____ and Thumper
jumped up.

Jimmy

Sunny

Skipper _____ .

slipped

stopped

Bump!

 Make complete sentences using the words from box A and box B.

Box A

Skipper

Skipper and Thumper

Jimmy and Skipper

Box B

bumped!

slipped.

jumped over.

Draw a line from each picture to the correct consonant blend. Fill in the blank.

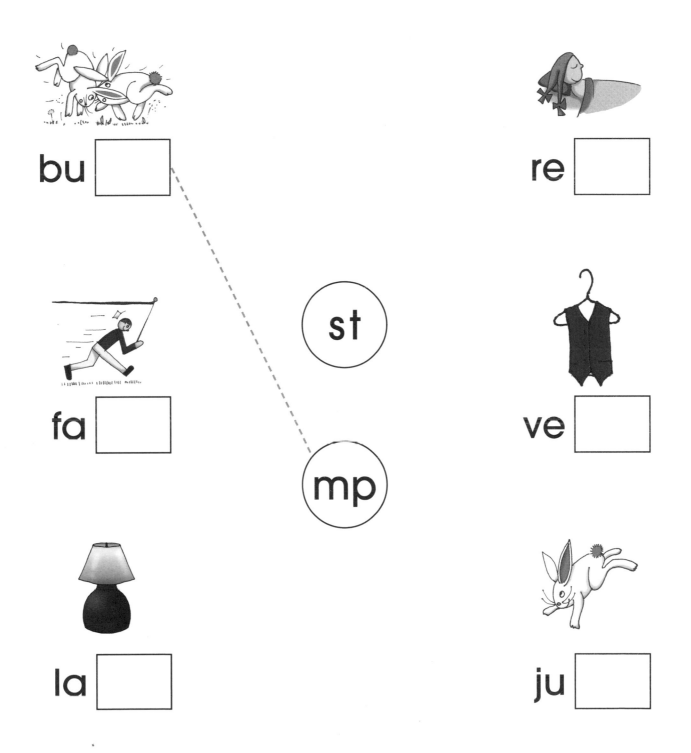

bu ☐

re ☐

st

fa ☐

ve ☐

mp

la ☐

ju ☐

Cat and Mouse

 Read the story and color each picture. Then circle the words in each sentence that have a short "a" sound, as in "apple."

Cat and Mouse

Tilly sat by the mouse house.

The mouse ran out of his house.

The cat went slam, slap, snap!

"Help! Help! Stop that cat!"

The mouse is happy to be back in his house.

 Say and write the words.

mouse <u>*mouse*</u>

house _____

kitty _____

sit _____

flip _____

skip _____

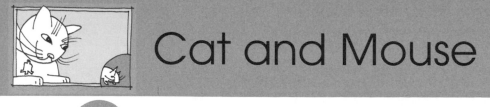

Cat and Mouse

Read each clue and complete the crossword.

Clues

1.
2.
3.
4.
5.
6.

Word Bank

mouse pond house kitty flip
fox   skip duck   sit   Jimmy

Fill in the missing letters to complete the sentence.

The cat is __ __ppy.

The cat __ __nt slam slap, snap!

The mouse is happy to be ba__ __ in his house.

"Help! He__ __! __ __op that cat!"

Tilly went __ __ip flop.

 Circle the words with the **short "a"** sound. Connect the circles to make a path.

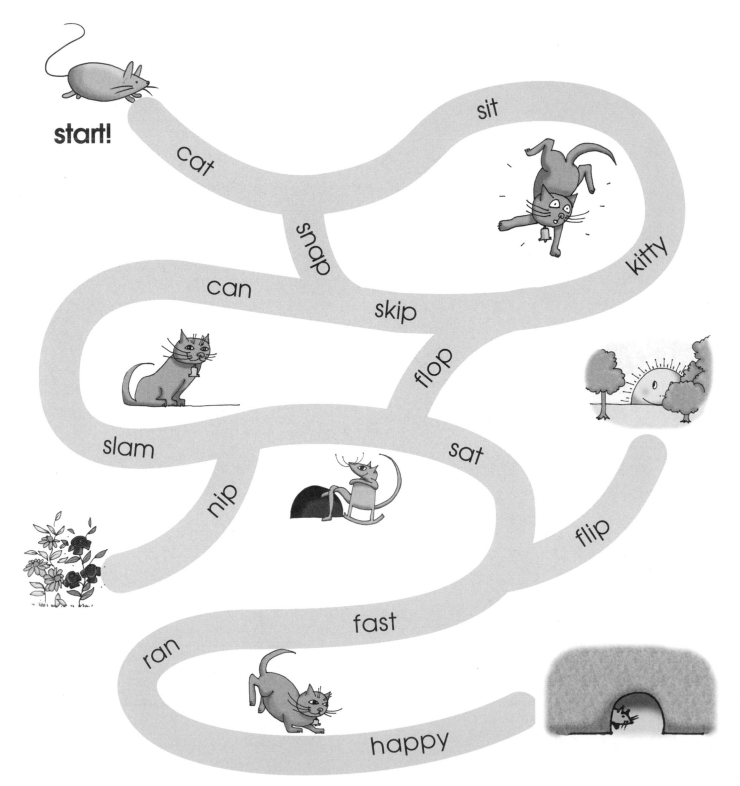

start!

cat

sit

snap

kitty

can

skip

slam

flop

nip

sat

flip

ran

fast

happy

 Draw a line to the correct word, then write it.

Tilly is a _____ cat.

happy

kitty

The _____ ran faster.

house

mouse

"Help! Help! _____ that cat!"

Stop

Step

Tilly went _____ flop.

flag

flip

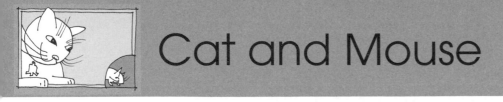

Cat and Mouse

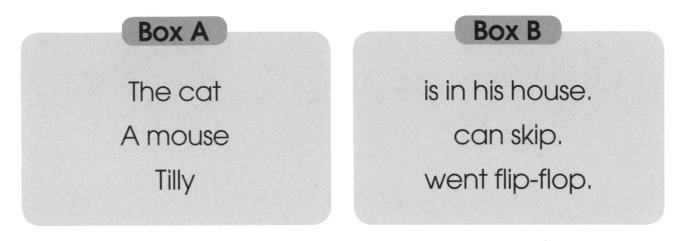

Make complete sentences using the words from box A and box B.

Box A

The cat

A mouse

Tilly

Box B

is in his house.

can skip.

went flip-flop.

Draw a line from each picture to the correct consonant blend. Fill in the blank.

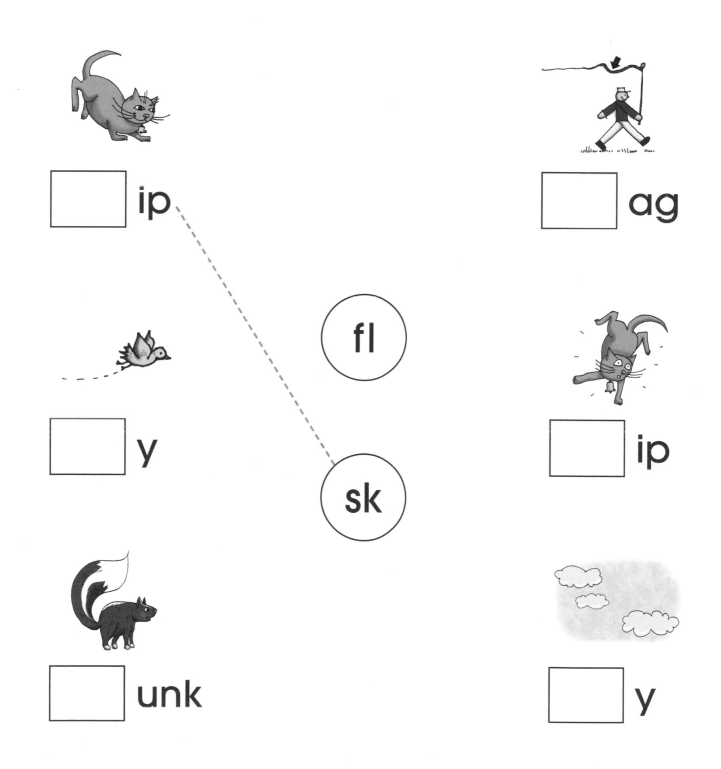

☐ ip

☐ ag

fl

☐ y

sk

☐ ip

☐ unk

☐ y

The Swimmers

 Read the story and color each picture. Then circle the words in each sentence that have a short "o" sound, as in "mop."

The Swimmers

It was summer. Pop, Stan, and Jim went to the pond.

Jim slipped into the pond. Stan jumped into the pond.

"Step on the log, Jim," called Stan. Jim slipped.

"Stop! Stop!" called Pop. The log spun.

The three swimmers went to a sunny spot.

Say and write the words.

swam <u>swam</u>

help

spun

slid

wet

sunny

The Swimmers

Read each clue and complete the crossword.

1
2
3
4
5
6

Word Bank

sunny	help	push	spun	swam
shop	slid	flew	wet	pal

Fill in the missing letters to complete the sentence.

Jim and Stan wanted to __ __im.

Jim __ __ipped into the pond.

Pop wanted to he__ __ Jim and Stan.

Stan __ __id.

" __ __ep on the log, Jim," called Stan.

The Swimmers

Circle the words with the **short "o"** sound.
Connect the circles to make a path.

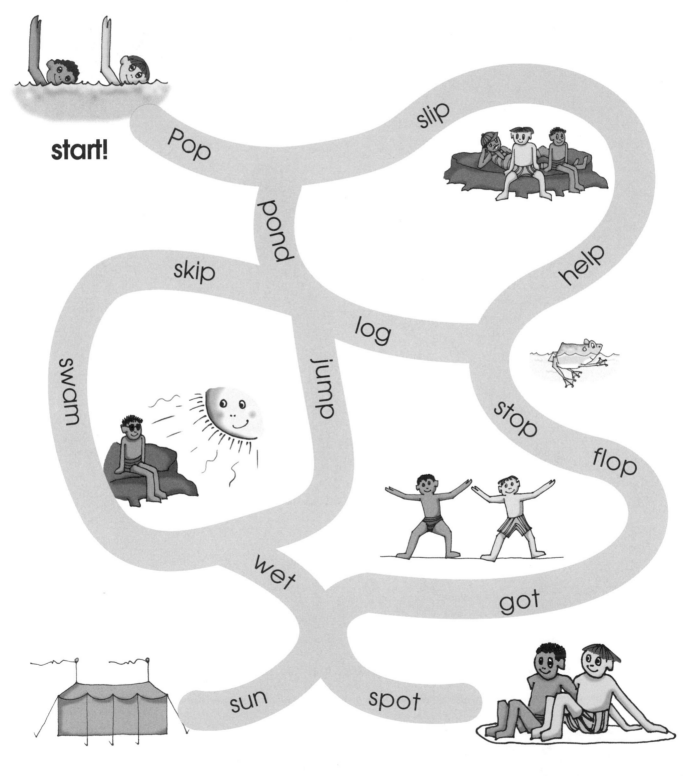

start!

Pop

slip

pond

skip

help

swam

log

jump

stop

flop

wet

got

sun

spot

 Draw a line to the correct word, then write it.

 Pop, Stan, and Jim

went to the _____ .

sand

pond

 Jim and Stan

_____ to a log.

swam

slid

 The log _____ .

spot

spun

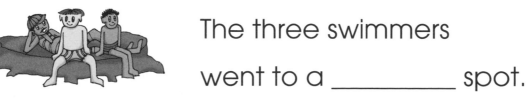 The three swimmers

went to a _____ spot.

sunny

funny

The Swimmers

 Make complete sentences using the words from box A and box B.

Box A

Pop

Jim and Stan

The log

Box B

spun.

swam to a log.

got wet.

Draw a line from each picture to the correct consonant blend. Fill in the blank.

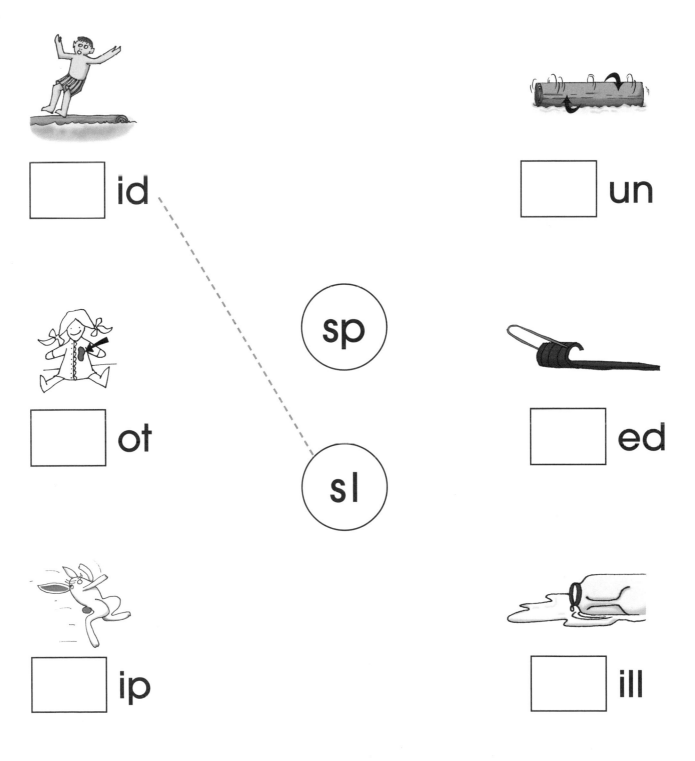

Samantha

 Read the story and color each picture. Then circle the words in each sentence that have a short "i" sound, as in "sit."

Samantha

Mama cooked eggs.

Toast popped from the toaster.

The smells whiffed into Samantha's room.

Her nose sniffed and sniffed. She licked her lips.

"Good morning," said the bright sunlight.

Match each word to the correct picture.

 smell

 sniff

morning

lick

bark

 tweet

Samantha

 Read each clue and complete the crossword.

Clues

①
②
③
④
⑤
⑥

Word Bank

morning   bed   smell   pup   sniff
toast   tweet   lip   bark   lick

Fill in the missing letters to complete the sentence.

The smells __ __iffed
into Samantha's room.

She li__ __ed her lips.

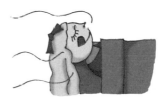

"Good mo__ __ing, Mama
and Papa," she said.

"Woof! Woof!" ba__ __ed
Roofus.

"Good morn__ __ __,"
said the bright sunlight.

 Circle the words ending with **"ed."**
Connect the circles to make a path.

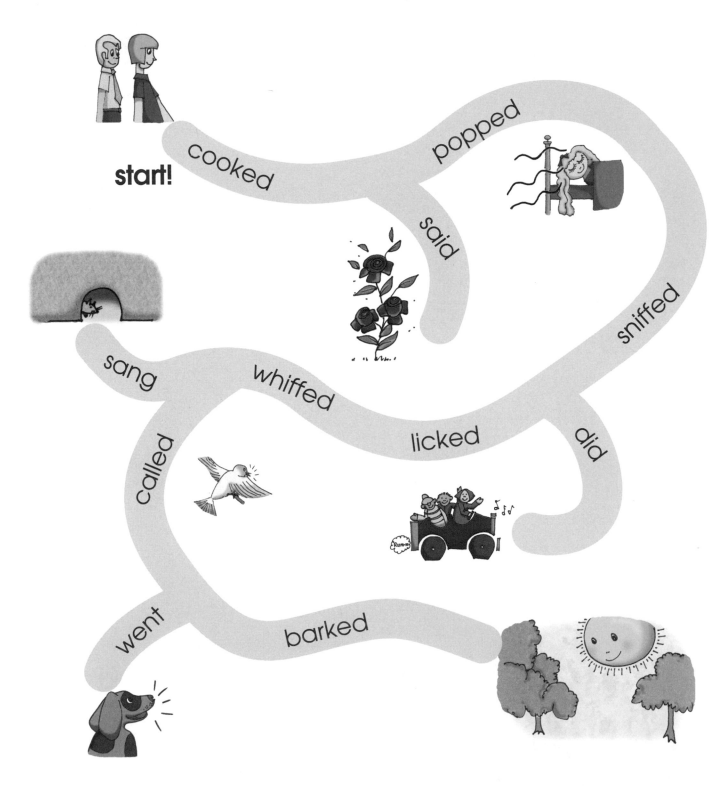

start!

cooked

popped

said

sniffed

sang

whiffed

licked

did

called

went

barked

118

Draw a line to the correct word, then write it.

 " _____ tight, Samantha," said Mama.

Sleep

Slap

Samantha was _____ in bed.

still

lost

"Woof! Woof!" _____ Roofus.

barked

started

 "Good _____," said the bright sunlight.

horn

morning

Put the words in the correct order to make the sentences.

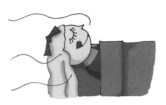

her   lips   licked   She

_____ ____ ____ l _____

h_____ ____ _____.

sun   The   set

____ ____ ____ s_____ ____ ____ ____.

eggs   Mama   cooked

_____ ____ ____ _____ ____ ____ ____

e _____ ____.

Circle and write the correct consonant blend for each picture.

| sm | ell |

st **sm** sk sl

ba ▢

rl lt rk lk

▢ iff

sp st sw sn

▢ eet

tw sw tr sr

Willy's Wish

 Read the story and color each picture. Then circle the words in each sentence that have a short "i" sound, as in "hit."

Willy's Wish

Willy threw three pennies into the wishing well.

Willy sat and sat. He put his chin on his hand. "I have a car. I have a cat."

"I have a card game. I have a jet plane. What can I wish?"

He sniffed and sniffed.

Willy said, "I wish, I wish," as he licked his lips, "for a big, big dish of FISH AND CHIPS!"

Match each word to the correct picture.

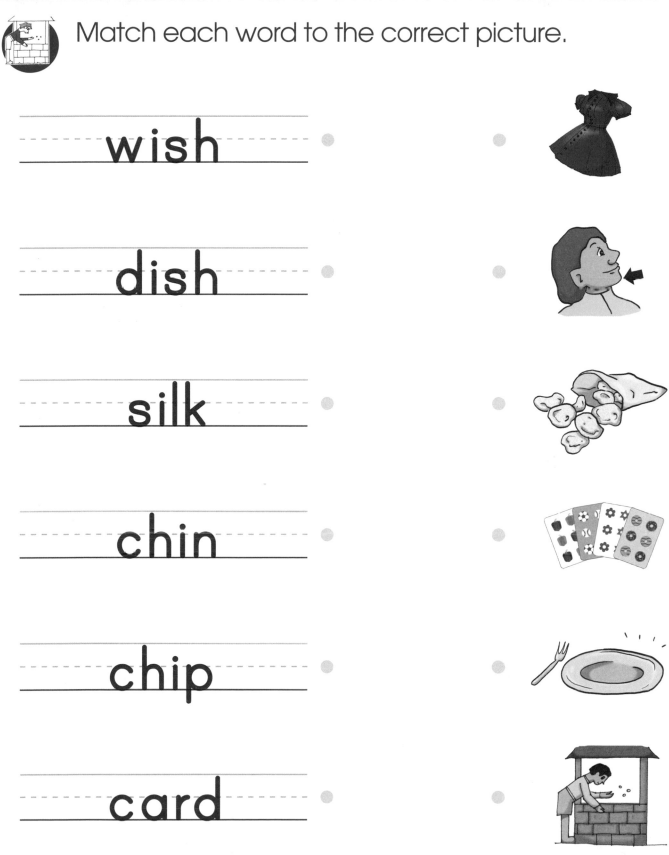

wish

dish

silk

chin

chip

card

Willy's Wish

Read each clue and complete the crossword.

Clues

1.
2.
3.
4.
5.
6.

Word Bank

chin   silk   well   dish   think
wish   card   cap   hand   chip

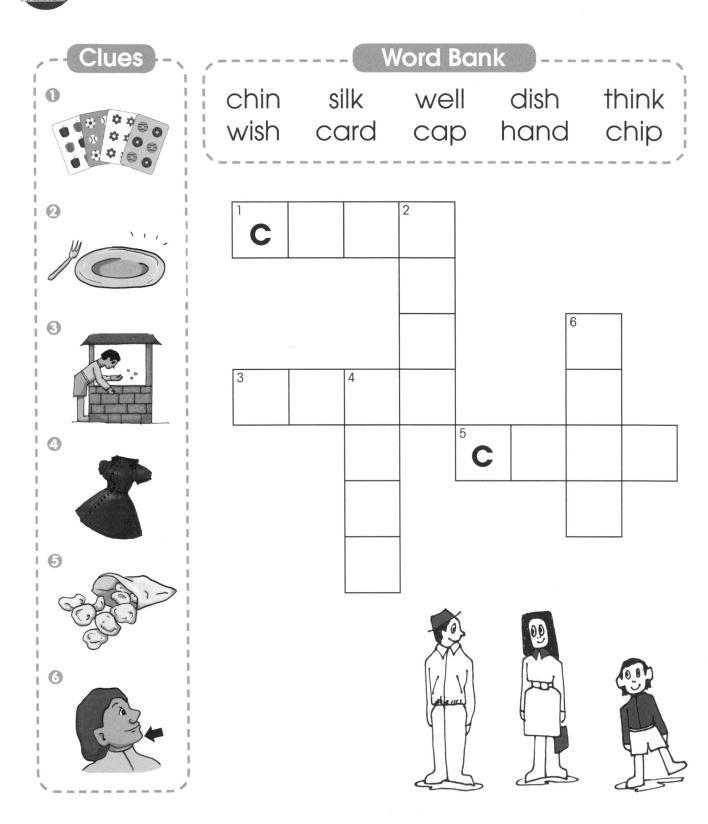

Fill in the missing letters to complete the sentence.

What do you wi__ __?

He put his __ __ in on
his hand.

I have a ca__ __ game.

Fish and __ __ips.

His mama wished for a
red si__ __ dress.

He li__ __ed his lips.

Willy's Wish

 Circle the words with the **short "i"** sound.
Connect the circles to make a path.

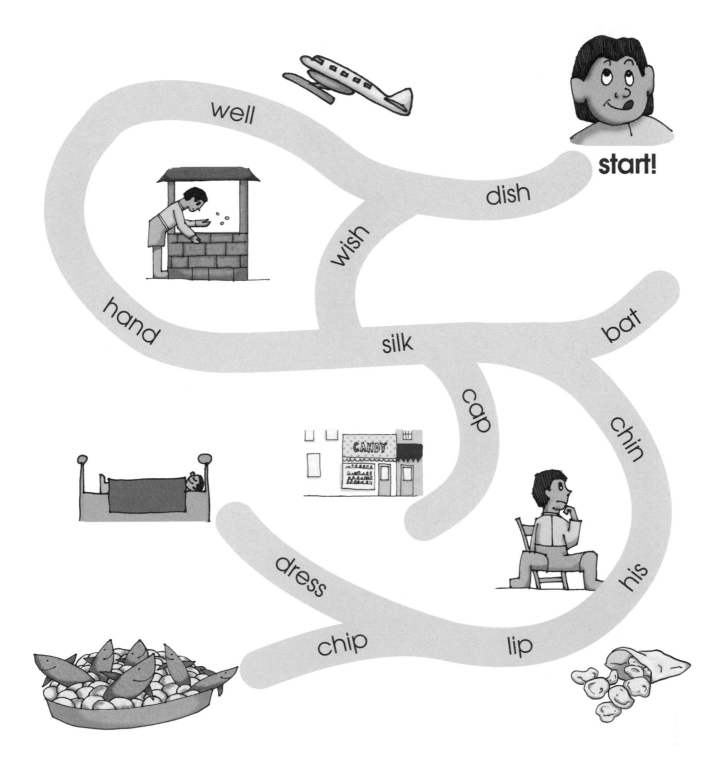

well

dish

start!

wish

hand

silk

bat

cap

chin

dress

chip

lip

his

126

Draw a line to the correct word, then write it.

 "What do you _____ ?" his mama said.

wish

fish

 "I cannot _____," is all he said.

threw

think

 He put his _____ on his hand.

chip

chin

 I have a _____ game.

card

car

Willy's Wish

 Put the words in the correct order to make the sentences.

a   I   plane   have   jet

_ h _ _ _   _   _ _ _

P_ _ _ _ _.

wish   do   What   you

_ _ _ _   _ _ _

w_ _ _?

lips   licked   He   his

_ _   _ _ _ _ _

h_ _ _ _ _.

Circle and write the correct consonant blend for each picture.

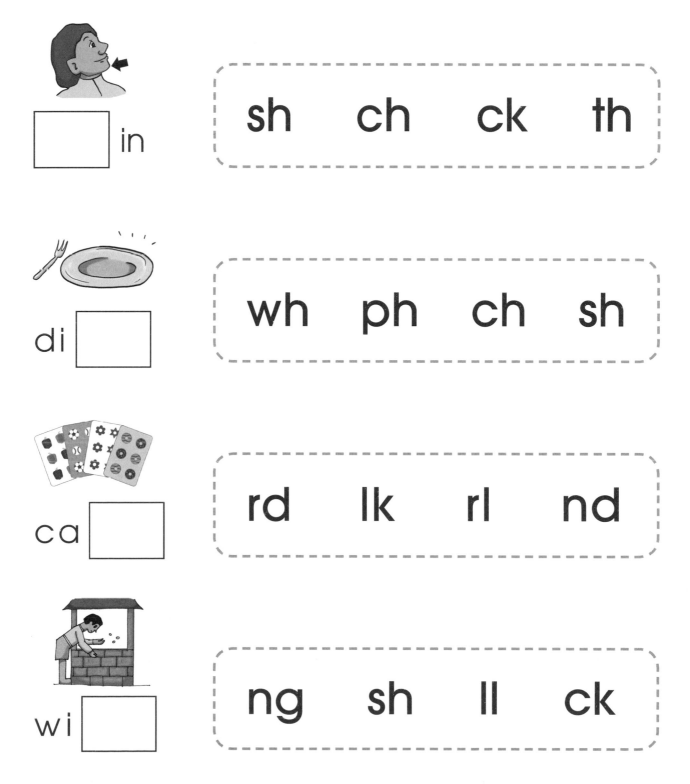

in

| sh | ch | ck | th |

di

| wh | ph | ch | sh |

ca

| rd | lk | rl | nd |

wi

| ng | sh | ll | ck |

 Read the story and color each picture. Then circle the words in each sentence that have a short "a" sound, as in "pat."

Jumper and the Clown

The clown had red pants with pink dots.

Her top was green and yellow.

Her hat had spots of blue and orange.

She had a round red nose and a big grin. Her hair was purple.

With the clown was a little brown and black pup.

Match each word to the correct picture.

clown •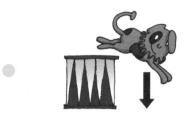

town •

brown •

grin •

down •

crown •

Read each clue and complete the crossword.

Clues

1.
2.
3.
4.
5.
6.

Word Bank

grin   play   crown   pink   town
down   clown   spot   brown   clap

Fill in the missing letters to complete the sentence.

A __ __own came to town!

Her top was __ __een and yellow.

With the clown was a little __ __own and __ __ack pup.

The clown grinned a big __ __in.

The clown had red pants with pi__ __ dots.

Jumper and the Clown

Circle the words with the **"ow"** sound.
Connect the circles to make a path.

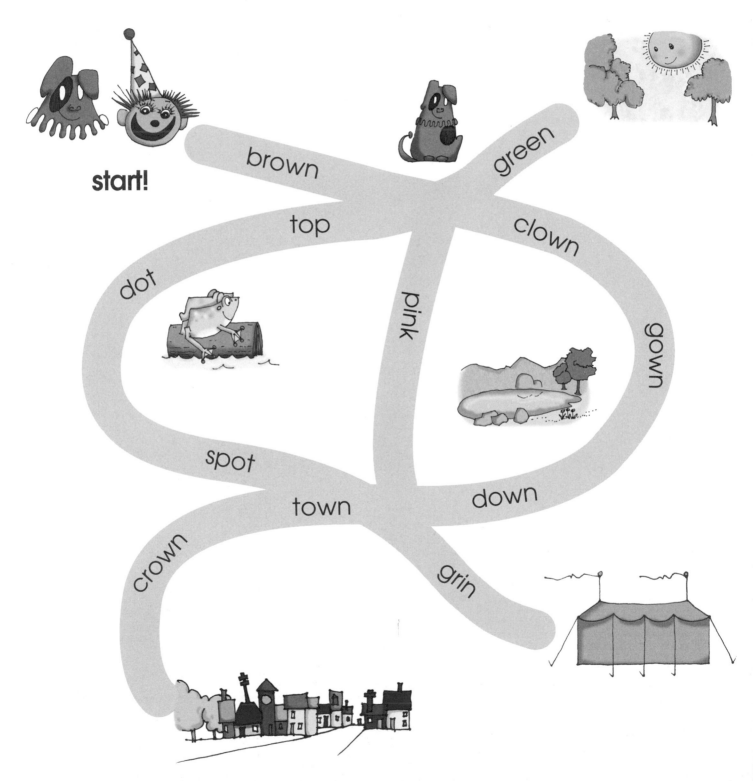

start!

brown

green

top

clown

dot

pink

gown

spot

town

down

crown

grin

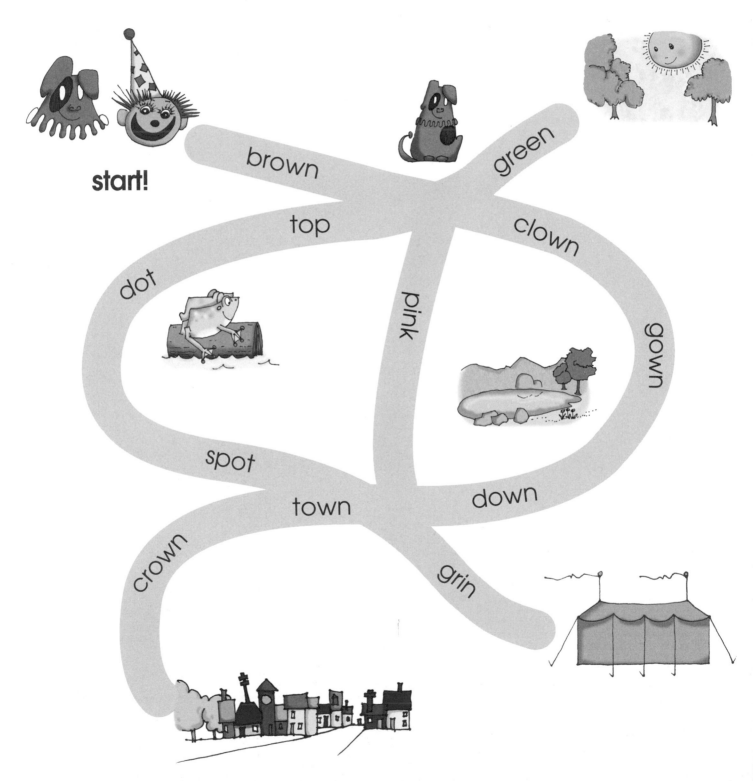

Draw a line to the correct word, then write it.

 A clown came to _____ !

frown

town

 She had a round red nose and a big _____ .

spin

grin

 With the clown was a little _____ and black pup.

brown

crown

 He jumped up.
He jumped _____ .

down

gown

Jumper and the Clown

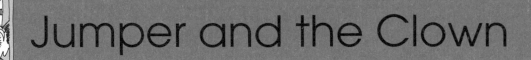 Put the words in the correct order to make the sentences.

hair   purple   Her   was

_ _ _   _ _   h_ _ _ _   _ _ _

P_ _ _ _ _ _ _ .

was   Jumper   pup   The   called

_ _ _   _ _ _   w_ _

_ _ _ _ _ _   _ _ _ _ _ _ _ _ .

clown   to   town   A   came

_   _ _ _ _ _   c_ _ _

_ _   _ _ _ _ !

Circle and write the correct consonant blend for each picture.

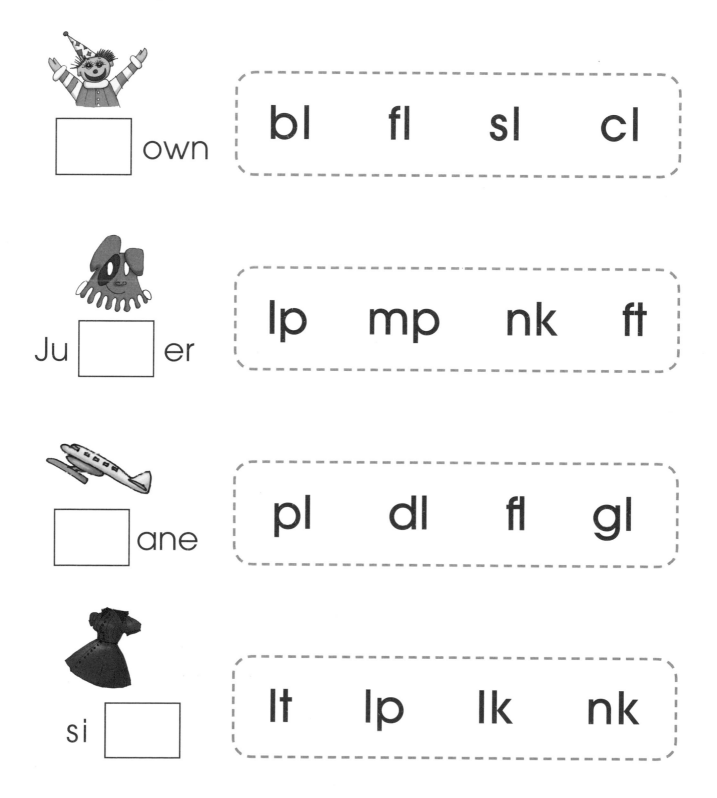

☐ own

| bl | fl | sl | cl |

Ju ☐ er

| lp | mp | nk | ft |

☐ ane

| pl | dl | fl | gl |

si ☐

| lt | lp | lk | nk |

 Read the story and color each picture. Then circle the words in each sentence that have a short "i" sound, as in "mit."

Max and the Tom Cats

Six tom cats sit on the tiptop of a big wall.

The sun will set soon.

Max, who is six, sits up in a tree.

"Hey, cats," calls Max, "what do you see?"

Max was glad he was in the tree to see the moonlight and to hear the song.

Match each word to the correct picture.

 tree •   •

 moon •   •

 look •   •

 light •   •

 night •   •

 bright •   •

Read each clue and complete the crossword.

Clues

❶
❷
❸
❹
❺
❻

Word Bank

light   glad   bright   last   night
look   moon   song   tree   white

Fill in the missing letters to complete the sentence.

Max, who is six, sits up in a tr__ __.

After a t__me the sun did set.

Max sat looking at the big wh__te moon.

The man in the m__ __n saw six cats and Max.

Goodni__ __ __, Max.
Goodni__ __ __, Cats.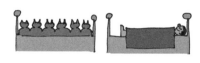

Max and the Tom Cats

 Circle the words with the silent **"gh."**
Connect the circles to make a path.

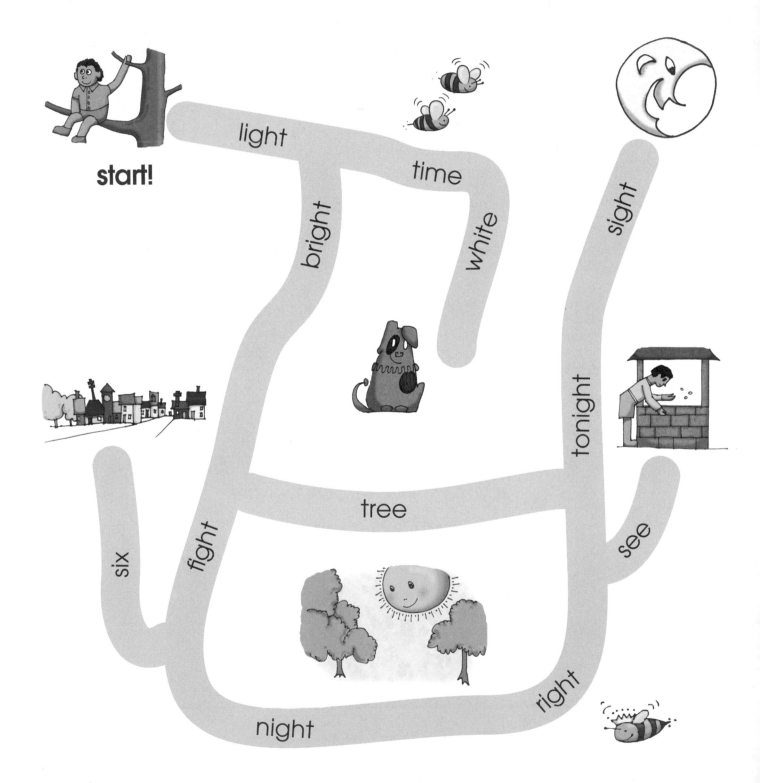

start!

light

time

bright

white

sight

tonight

tree

fight

see

six

night

right

142

Draw a line to the correct word, then write it.

Max, who is six,

sits up in a _____ .

tree

see

The man in the _____

saw six cats and Max.

soon

moon

Soon the bright _____

of the moon sat over

them all.

light

sight

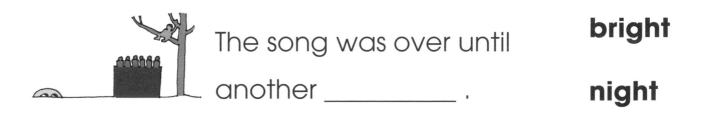

The song was over until

another _____ .

bright

night

 Put the words in the correct order to make the sentences.

to   bed   Max   Go

G_____   ___ ___   ___ ___,

M___.

soon   will   sun   The   set

___ ___ ___ ___   w___ ___ ___

___ ___ ___ ___.

do   see   What   you

W___ ___ ___

___ ___ ___ ___ ___?

Circle and write the correct consonant blend for each picture.

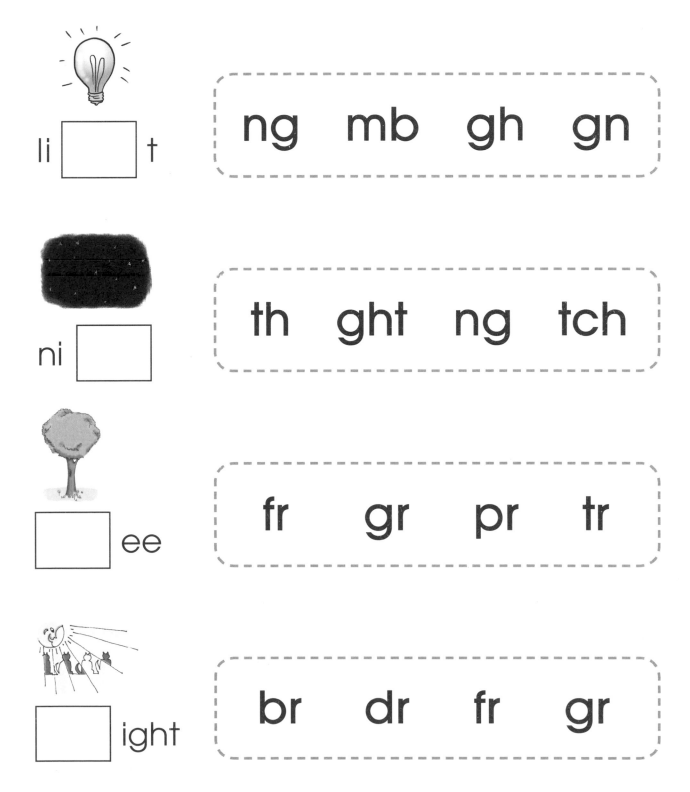

li ☐ t

ng   mb   gh   gn

ni ☐

th   ght   ng   tch

☐ ee

fr   gr   pr   tr

☐ ight

br   dr   fr   gr

I read it!

Complex Words

1. ☐ Ten Men

2. ☐ Bump!

3. ☐ Cat and Mouse

4. ☐ The Swimmers

5. ☐ Samantha

6. ☐ Willy's Wish

7. ☐ Jumper and the Clown

8. ☐ Max and the Tom Cats

My Book Report

Name: _____ **Date:** _____

Name
The title of my book is...

Characters
The main characters are...

Book Rating
I give the book...

☆ ☆ ☆ ☆ ☆

Setting
This story takes place in...

Beginning

Middle

End

My favorite part of the book is...

_____

_____

_____

Make a copy of this page for each of the books in the set.

"I read the whole book!"

BOB BOOKS
Complex Words

_____

Name

BOB BOOKS®

Long Vowels

Workbook
Activities

The Game

The Game

Kate was playing first base.
Dave threw the ball to Kate,

Jane made it to base.
Jane was safe on first
base.

James hit the ball hard.

Kate got the ball.
She threw it to the base.

The ball game went on
and on. The game went
on until the sun set.

154

Say and write the words. Circle the letter that says its name, then cross out the silent letter.

game   g(a)m~~e~~

Jane

base

Kate

safe

gave

The Game

Circle and match the beginning letter to complete the correct word.

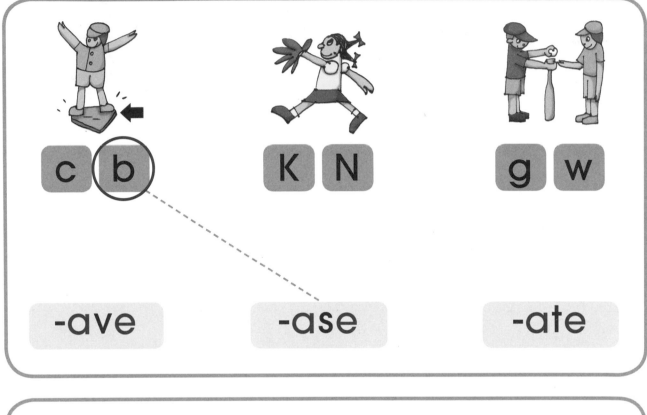

c (b)   K N   g w

-ave   -ase   -ate

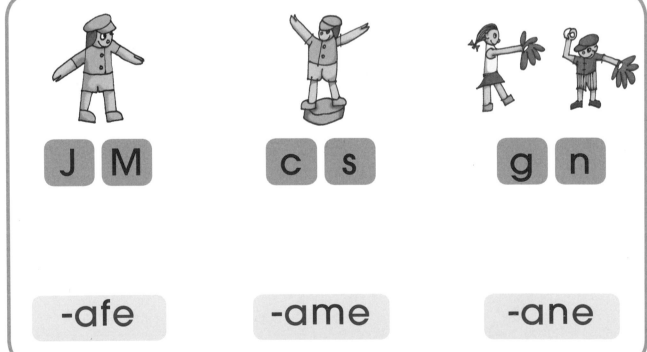

J M   c s   g n

-afe   -ame   -ane

Circle the word that goes with the picture, then write the word on the line.

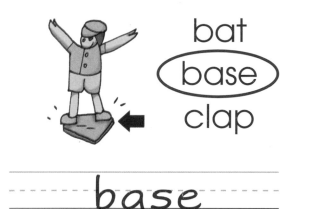

bat

(base)

clap

base

Jane

van

clam

cap

Kate

jar

Kate

safe

made

fan

gave

make

game

mat

ham

The Game

Read each sentence. Find the word that is wrong and write it in the red box. Write the correct word in the orange box.

Jane was (save) on first base.

| save | ⟶ | safe |

The ball gam went on and on.

| | ⟶ | |

Jane took the ball and bate.

| | ⟶ | |

She threw it to the bake.

| | ⟶ | |

Make complete sentences using the words from the box.

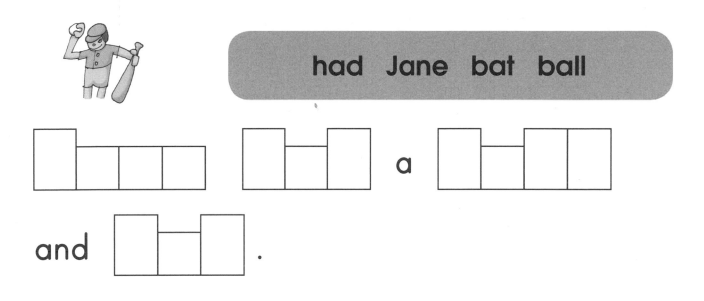

had   Jane   bat   ball

☐☐☐☐   ☐☐☐ a ☐☐☐☐

and ☐☐☐ .

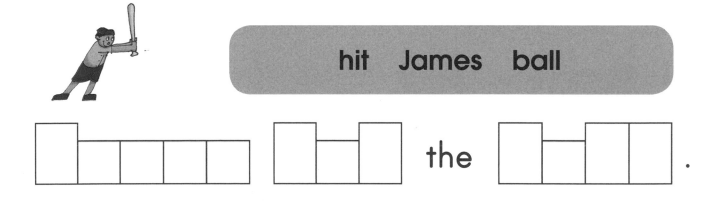

hit   James   ball

☐☐☐☐   ☐☐☐ the ☐☐☐☐ .

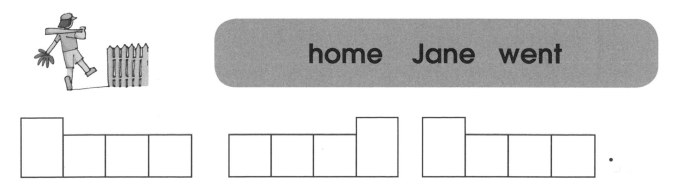

home   Jane   went

☐☐☐☐   ☐☐☐☐   ☐☐☐☐ .

The Game

Kate got the ball. She threw it to the base.

Jane made it to the base. Jane was safe on first base.

Jane took the ball and bat. Jane went home.

Kate was playing first base. Dave threw the ball to Kate.

Jake threw the ball over the plate. James hit the ball hard.

Look at each picture and fill in the missing vowel for each word.

c <u>a</u> t

c <u>a</u> k <u>e</u>

b __ t

b __ s __

g __ m __

h __ t

f __ st

pl __ n __

Joe's Toe

Read the story and color each picture. Then circle the words in each sentence that have a long "o" sound, as in "home."

Joe's Toe

Joe rode his bike over a bump.

The bike hit a stone. Joe lost control of the bike.

It bumped into a pole. Poor Joe had a jolt!

He broke his bike. He broke his big toe.

Sam took Joe to the doctor. The doctor fixed the broken toe.

Say and write the words. Circle the letter that says its name, then cross out the silent letter.

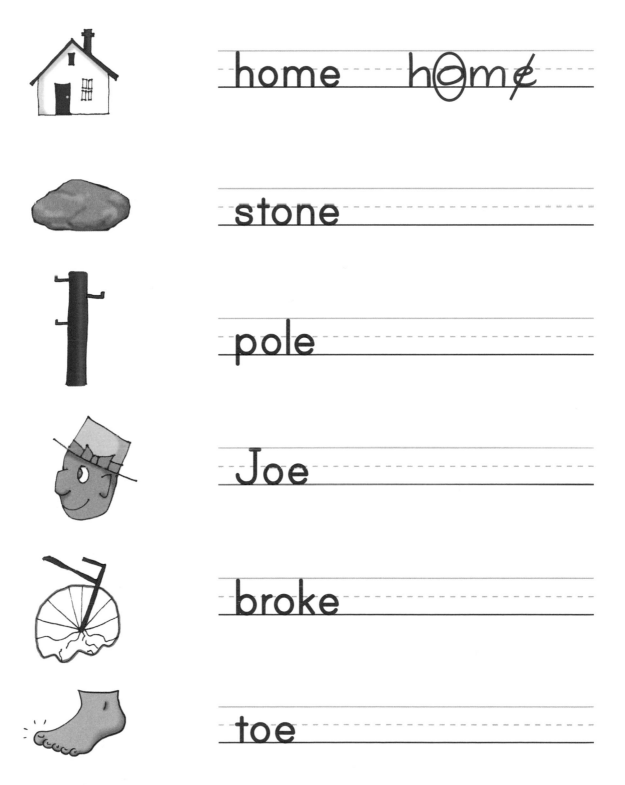

home   hⓞmé

stone

pole

Joe

broke

toe

 Circle and match the beginning letter to complete the correct word.

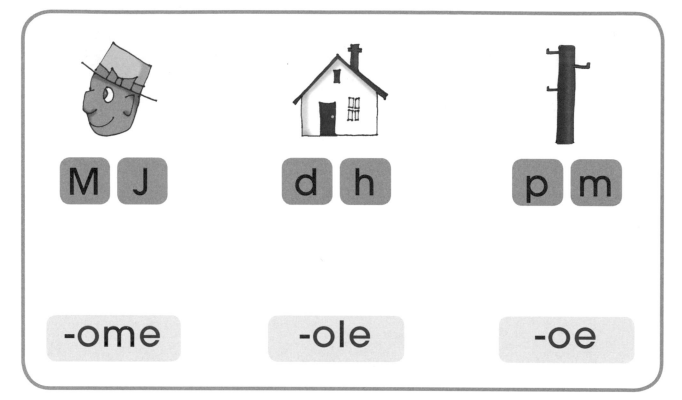

M J   d h   p m

-ome   -ole   -oe

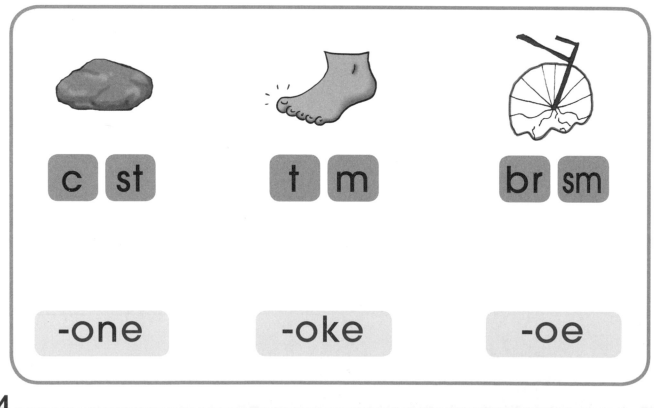

c st   t m   br sm

-one   -oke   -oe

Circle the word that goes with the picture, then write the word on the line.

top
(home)
frog

home

stone
pop
shop

_____

pot
pole
flop

_____

doe
goes
Joe

_____

stone
broke
pole

_____

tea
toe
tree

_____

165

Joe's Toe

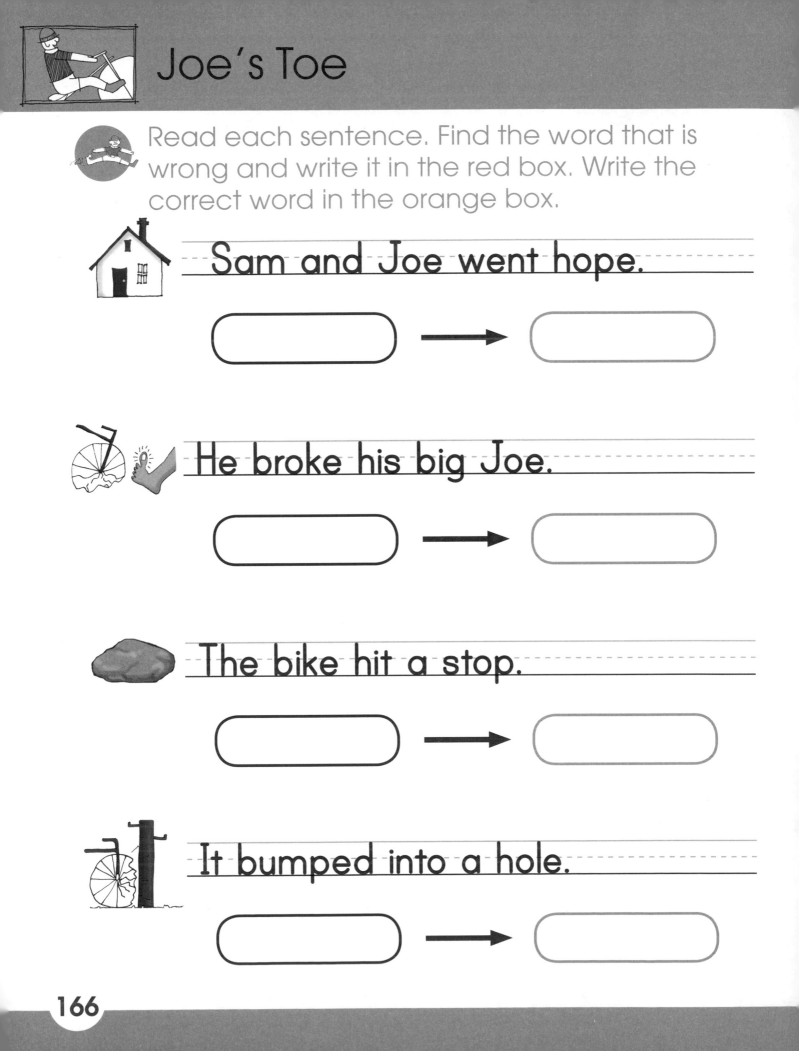

Read each sentence. Find the word that is wrong and write it in the red box. Write the correct word in the orange box.

Sam and Joe went hope.

He broke his big Joe.

The bike hit a stop.

It bumped into a hole.

Bob Books Long Vowels

 Make complete sentences using the words from the box.

his   broke   He   bike

hit   bike   stone

The _____ _____ a _____ .

good   found   tool   Sam

_____ _____ a _____ .

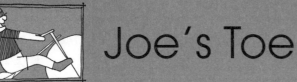

Read each sentence, then draw a line to the correct picture.

Joe rode his bike over a bump.

He went head over heels.

He broke his big toe.

The doctor fixed the broken toe.

Sam fixed the broken bike.

Look at each picture and fill in the missing vowel for each word.

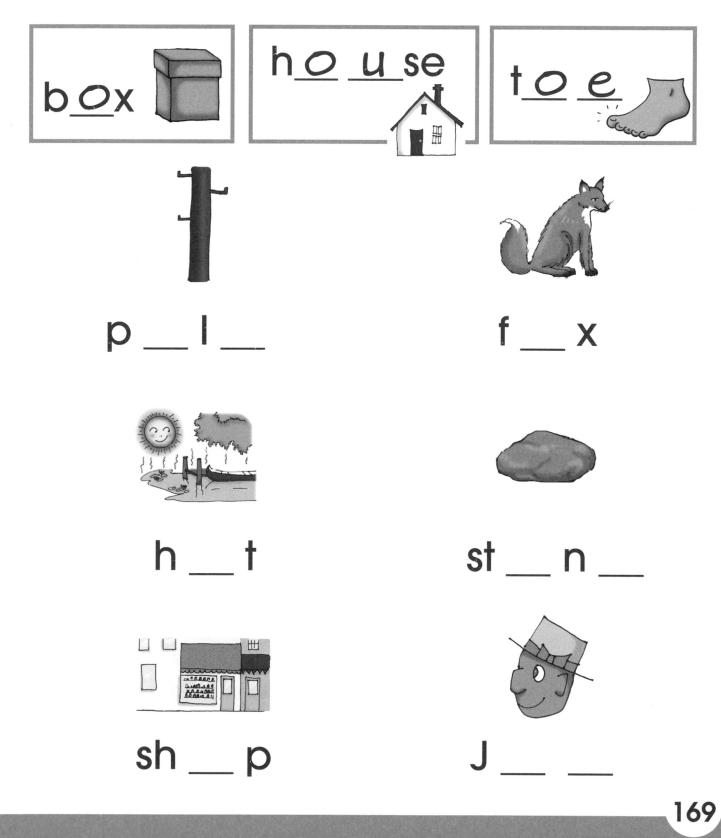

b _o_ x

h _o_ u _ se

t _o_ e

p __ l __

f __ x

h __ t

st __ n __

sh __ p

J __ __

Bud's Nap

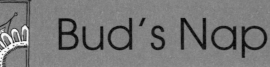

Read the story and color each picture. Then circle the words in each sentence that have a long "e" sound, as in "me."

Bud's Nap

Bud sat under a big green tree. Bud was sleepy.

Three bees buzzed and the queen bee buzzed.

A bee sat on Bud's knee.

A butterfly sat on Bud's nose.

Bud jumped up. He did not feel sleepy anymore.

Complete each word with **"ee."** Then write and read the whole word.

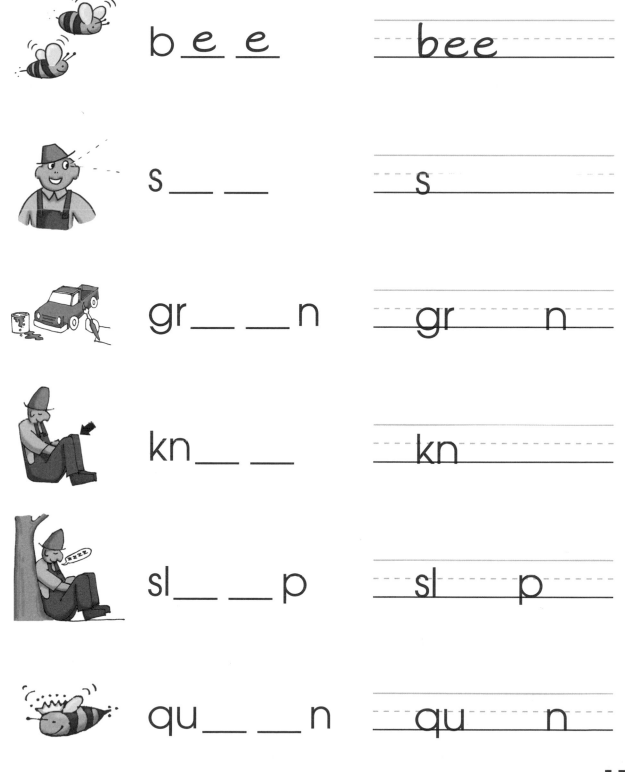

b e e   bee

s _ _   s

gr _ _ n   gr   n

kn _ _   kn

sl _ _ p   sl   p

qu _ _ n   qu   n

Bud's Nap

Draw a line to connect the correct letters, then write the word.

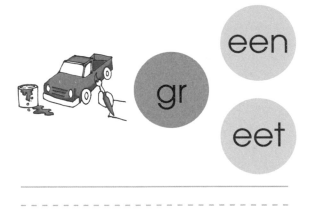

sl — eep

im

sleep

b — ee

y

gr — een

eet

kn — it

ee

s — ea

ee

qu — ail

een

Find and color three pictures in a row with the same sound. Say the picture names.

short "e" sound, as in "bed."

long "e" sound, as in "sleep."

Bud's Nap

Read each sentence. Find the word that is wrong and write it in the red box. Write the correct word in the orange box.

Bud sat under a big grin tree.

[ ] → [ ]

The quick bee buzzed.

[ ] → [ ]

Bud did not sea the bees.

[ ] → [ ]

He did not fill sleepy anymore.

[ ] → [ ]

Make complete sentences using the words from the box.

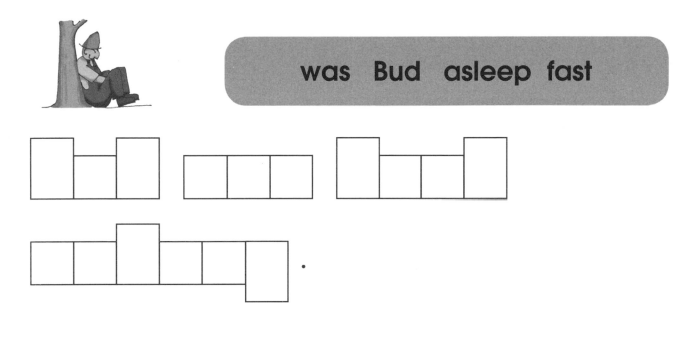

was Bud asleep fast

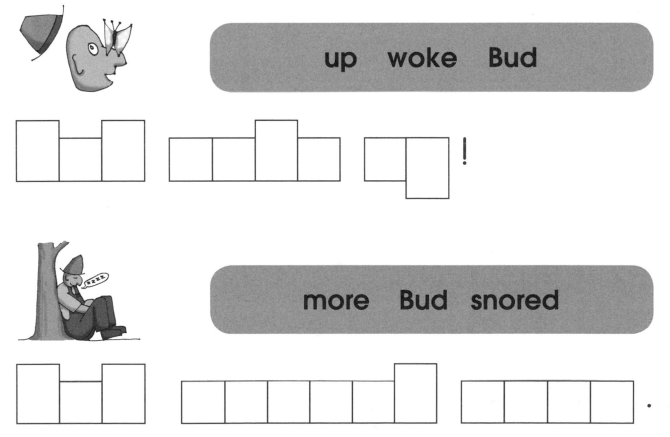

up woke Bud

more Bud snored

Bud's Nap

 Read each sentence, then draw a line to the correct picture.

The bees saw Bud sitting under the tree.

Three bees buzzed and the queen bee buzzed.

A bee sat on Bud's hand.

The butterfly sat on Bud's nose.

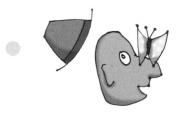

The butterfly flew into the sky.

 Look at each picture and fill in the missing vowel for each word.

b <u>e</u> d

tr <u>e</u> <u>e</u>

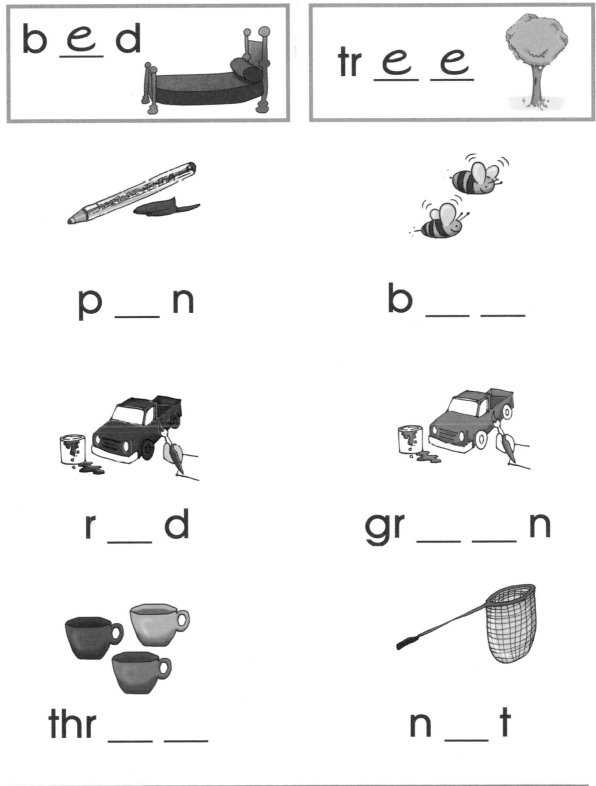

p __ n

b __ __

r __ d

gr __ __ n

thr __ __

n __ t

The Picnic

The Picnic

Jill had hot dogs, buns, green peas, and beans.

She had meatballs and peanut butter.

She put the hot tea into a teapot.

She put the picnic in a basket.

It was a treat to eat a picnic at the beach.

178

Complete each word with **"ea."** Then write and read the whole word.

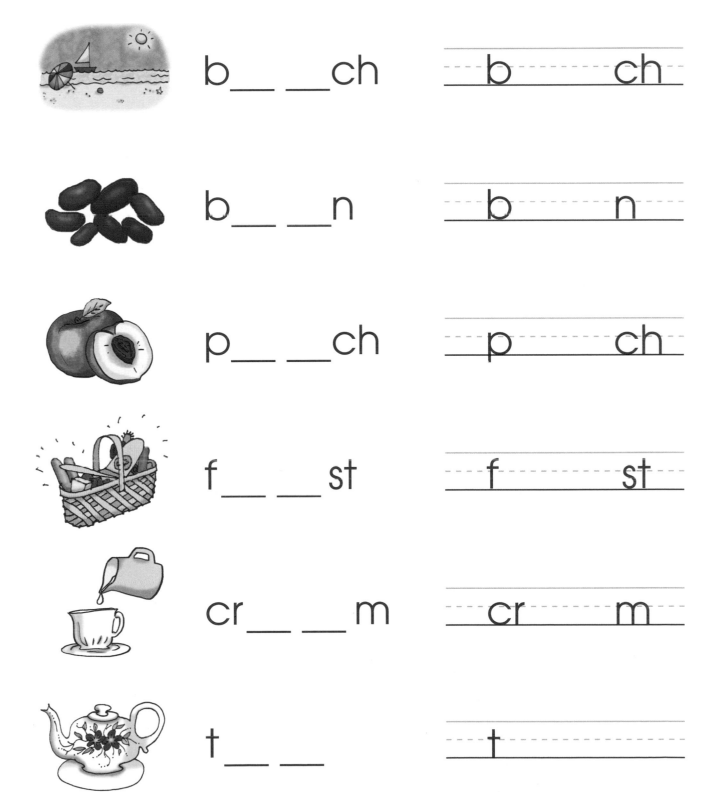

b__ __ch   b   ch

b__ __n   b   n

p__ __ch   p   ch

f__ __st   f   st

cr__ __m   cr   m

t__ __   t

The Picnic

 Draw a line to connect the correct letters.

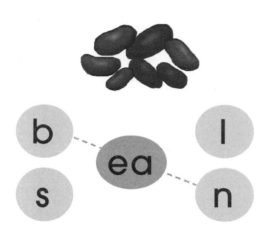

b   l

ea

s   n

l   ch

ea

b   sh

m   t

ea

f   st

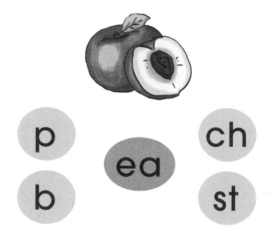

p   ch

ea

b   st

t

f   ea

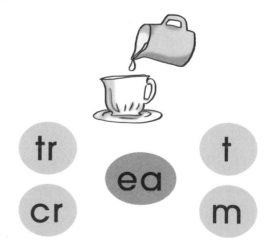

tr   t

ea

cr   m

Circle the word that goes with the picture, then write the word on the line.

bee
beach
left

_____

bean
less
tea

_____

beach
bean
peach

_____

knee
feast
peach

_____

cream
meet
shell

_____

tree
feed
tea

_____

The Picnic

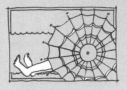

 Read each sentence. Find the word that is wrong and write it in the red box. Write the correct word in the orange box.

Jill made hot tee.

It was time to eat the fist.

Jill went to the beech.

They sipped tea by the see.

Make complete sentences using the words from the box.

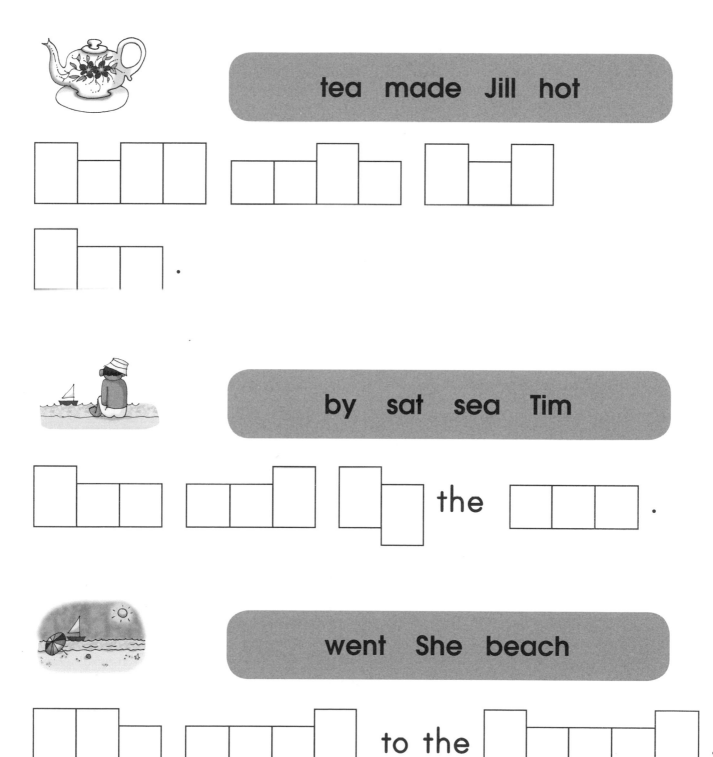

tea   made   Jill   hot

by   sat   sea   Tim

the

went   She   beach

to the

The Picnic

 Read each sentence, then draw a line to the correct picture.

Jill fixed a big picnic.

Jill had green peas and beans.

Jill had meatballs and peanut butter.

Jill put the hot tea into a teapot.

It was a treat to swim in the chilly sea.

Look at each picture and fill in the missing vowel for each word.

h _e_ n

l _e_ a f

t __ __ pot

l __ g

v __ t

b __ __ n

b __ __ ch

m __ n

 Read the story and color each picture. Then circle the words in each sentence that have a long "a" sound, as in "main."

The Train

The little train was painted black.

The little train ran in the rain.

The cow just stood and looked and wagged her tail.

Soon a little maid came along with a shiny pail.

As the cow wagged her tail, the maid pumped milk into the pail.

 Read and write the words.

t r | ai | n

train

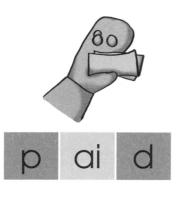

p | ai | d

_____

r | ai | n

_____

p | ai | l

_____

m | ai | d

_____

t | ai | l

_____

The Train

 Draw a line to connect the correct letters.

p — ai — d
w   i

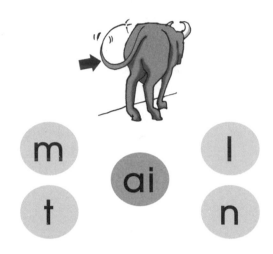

m   l
    ai
t   n

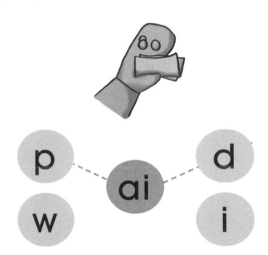

br   d
    ai
tr   n

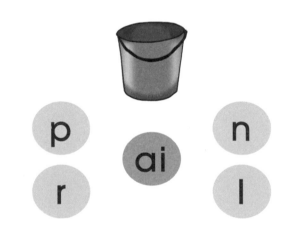

p   n
    ai
r   l

m   d
    ai
s   l

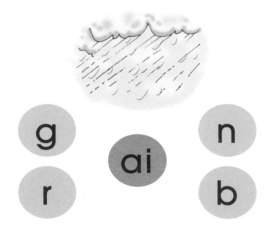

g   n
    ai
r   b

Unscramble the letters and write the word.
Draw a line to the correct picture.

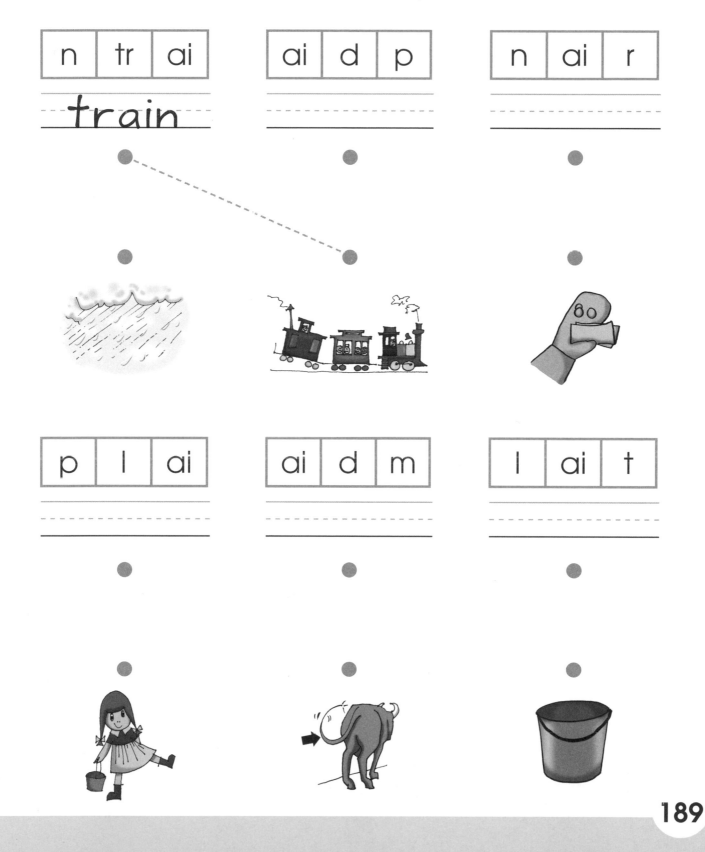

n	tr	ai

train

ai	d	p

n	ai	r

p	l	ai

ai	d	m

l	ai	t

189

The Train

 Read each sentence. Find the word that is wrong and write it in the red box. Write the correct word in the orange box.

The little tray was painted black.

The little train ran in the pain.

The cow was not awake.

A little maid came along with a tail.

Write complete sentences using the words from the boxes.

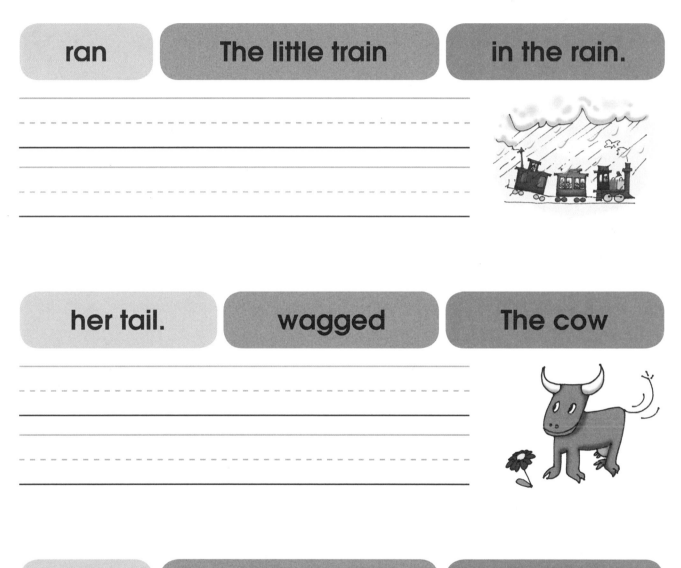

ran   The little train   in the rain.

_____

_____

her tail.   wagged   The cow

_____

_____

ran   up the hill.   The train

_____

_____

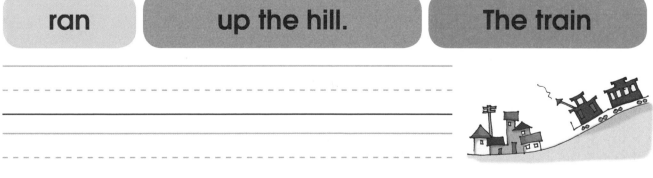

The Train

The little train ran in the rain.

It ran up the hill and down the hill.

On the track was a big brown cow.

A little maid came along with a shiny pail.

The maid pumped milk into the pail.

Look at each picture and color the correct vowel.

The Visit

 Read the story and color each picture. Then circle the words in each sentence that have a long "o" sound, as in "bone."

The Visit

A mouse had a house in a stone wall.

Mouse had a white phone. Toad had a red phone.

He put on his green coat and red slippers.

All the drivers were speeding past.

She took white paint and a big red card.

 Read and write the words.

r o ck

tr u ck

ph o n e

t oa d

r oa d

c oa t

The Visit

Fill in the missing letters. Draw a line to the matching picture.

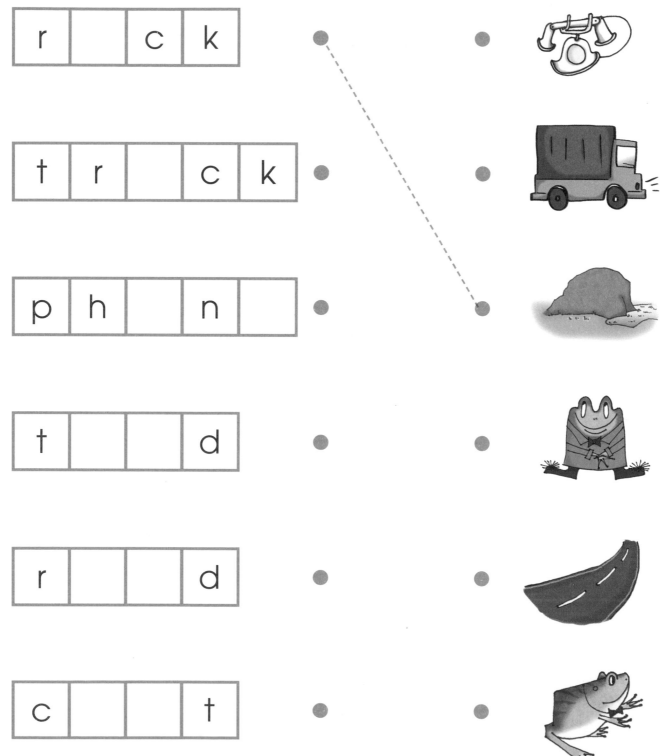

r		c	k

t	r		c	k

p	h		n	

t			d

r			d

c			t

196

Find and color three pictures in a row with the same sound. Say the picture names.

long "o_e" sound, as in "home."

long "oa" sound, as in "road."

The Visit

 Read each sentence. Find the word that is wrong and write it in the red box. Write the correct word in the orange box.

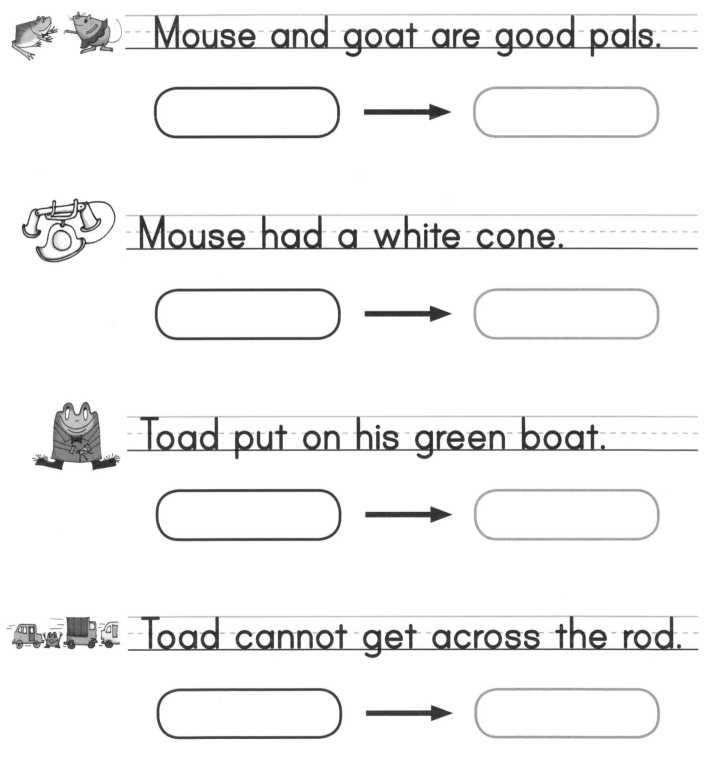

Mouse and goat are good pals.

Mouse had a white cone.

Toad put on his green boat.

Toad cannot get across the rod.

Write complete sentences using the words from the boxes.

had   Toad   a red phone.

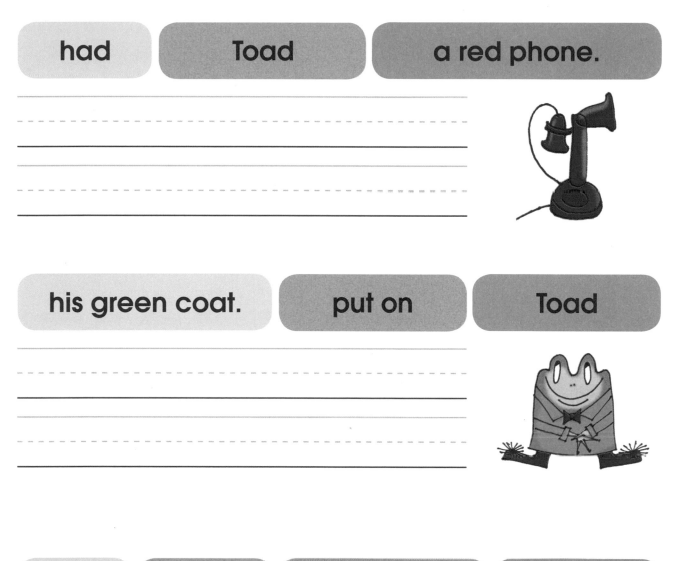

his green coat.   put on   Toad

waved   Mouse   up and down.   the sign

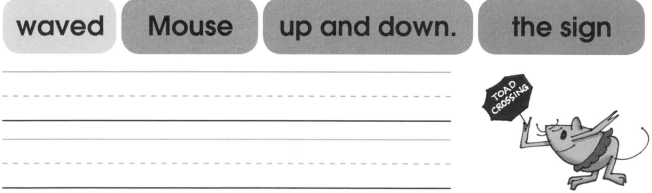

The Visit

A mouse had a house in a stone wall.

Toad had a red phone.

All the drivers were speeding past.

Toad sang a little tune.

Toad put a tiny foot into the street.

Look at each picture and color the correct vowel.

b o x

g o a t

Chickens

 Read the story and color each picture. Then circle the words in each sentence that have a "cr," "ch," or "cl" sound, as in "crack," "chip," or "clap."

Chickens

Chicken Big and Chicken Little had two chairs, a big chair and a little chair.

"Let us play a game," they said. "One, two, three, GO!"

Chicken Big sat in the little chair.

Chicken Little cheered and clapped her wings.

But all of a sudden, the little chair creaked, croaked, and broke!

Fill in the missing letters and write the words.

| ai | ea | i | a | ee | a |

ch ( ) se _____

ch ( ) r _____

cr ( ) sh _____

ch ( ) r _____

ch ( ) cken _____

cr ( ) k _____

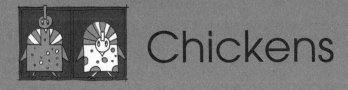
 Draw a line to complete the word and fill in the missing letters.

cr		
ch	air	

c h air

cr
ch
ase

__ __ase

cr
ch
ash

__ __ash

cr
ch
icken

__ __icken

cr
ch
eer

__ __eer

cr
ch
eak

__ __eak

Circle the word that goes with the picture,
then write the word on the line.

chase
case
chain

_____

chain
chair
care

_____

cheer
cheap
chew

_____

craim
crash
crack

_____

chicken
child
chilly

_____

cream
creek
creak

_____

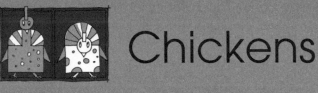
 Read each sentence. Find the word that is wrong and write it in the red box. Write the correct word in the orange box.

 Chicken Little sat in the big fair.

⟶

 Let us say a game!

⟶

She nodded her heed.

⟶

Chicken Big chosed Chicken Little across the room.

⟶

Write complete sentences using the words from the boxes.

| in the big chair. | Chicken Little | sat |

| clapped | her wings. | Chicken Big |

| her wings. | Chicken Big | checked |

Read each sentence, then draw a line to the correct picture.

Chicken Big chased Chicken Little across the room.

Chicken Little sat in the big chair.

Chicken Big cheered and clapped her wings.

She nodded her head.

Chicken Little ran to the big chair.

Look at each picture and color the correct consonant blend.

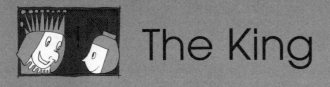

Read the story and color each picture. Then circle the words in each sentence that have an "ng" sound, as in "sing."

The King

In the spring, the king sang a ringing song.

She did not smile. She did not like his song.

The king did not feel happy. He did not feel proud.

So the little girl went to see the king.

"Now at last we are friends," said the king with a grin.

Read and write the words.

b a ng

s i ng

k i ng

r i ng

wr o ng

str o ng

Draw a line to complete the word and fill in the missing letters.

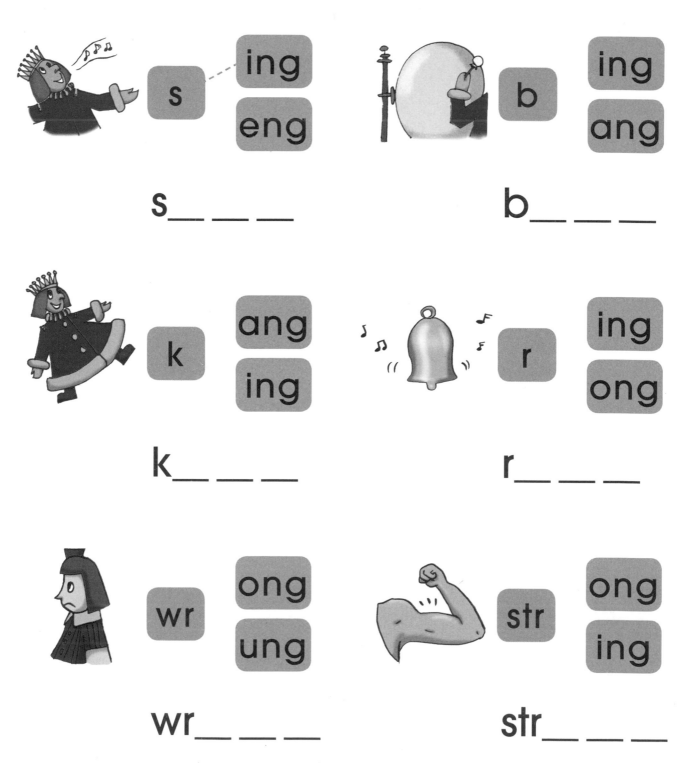

s | ing / eng

s__ __ __

b | ing / ang

b__ __ __

k | ang / ing

k__ __ __

r | ing / ong

r__ __ __

wr | ong / ung

wr__ __ __

str | ong / ing

str__ __ __

Unscramble the letters and write the word.
Draw a line to the correct picture.

| i | s | ng |

_____

| wr | ng | o |

_____

| ng | r | i |

_____

| a | ng | b |

_____

| i | k | ng |

_____

| ng | o | str |

_____

The King

Read each sentence. Find the word that is wrong and write it in the red box. Write the correct word in the orange box.

She did not like his long.

The sing did not feel happy.

The bell did bring.

He spoke in a tone very string.

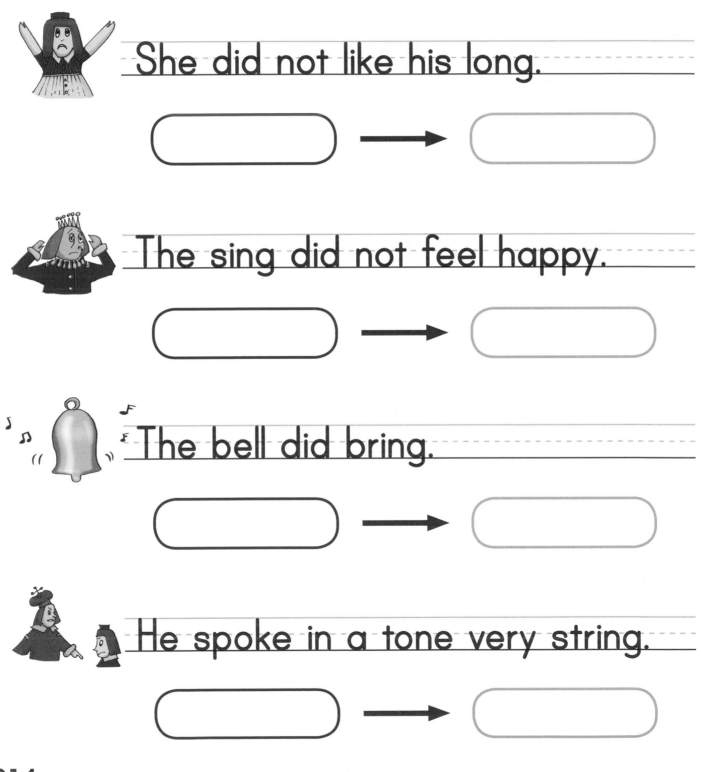

Write complete sentences using the words from the boxes.

in the spring.	was	The king	happy

sang	the song.	The girl

her foot.	She	stamped

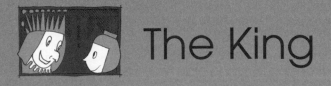

 Read each sentence, then draw a line to the correct picture.

The little girl went to see the king.

The king sang a ringing song.

The king was happy in the spring.

The girl frowned and stamped her foot.

The king went to bed.

Look at each picture and color the correct blends.

ang	ang
ing	ing
ong	ong

ang	ang
ing	ing
ong	ong

ang	ang
ing	ing
ong	ong

I read it!

Long Vowels

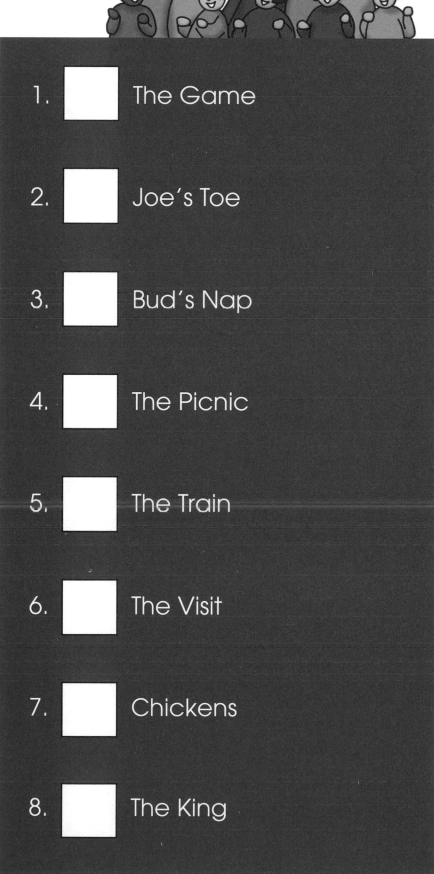

1. ☐ The Game

2. ☐ Joe's Toe

3. ☐ Bud's Nap

4. ☐ The Picnic

5. ☐ The Train

6. ☐ The Visit

7. ☐ Chickens

8. ☐ The King

My Book Report

Name: _____ **Date:** _____

Name
The title of my book is...

Characters
The main characters are...

Book Rating
I give the book

☆ ☆ ☆ ☆ ☆

Setting
This story takes place in...

Beginning

→

Middle

→

End

My favorite part of the book is...

_____

_____

Make a copy of this page for each of the books in the set.

"I read the
whole book!"

BOB BOOKS
Long Vowels

_____
Name

BOB
BOOKS